INTO THE OBLIVION

THE 66TH REBIRTH OF FRANKIE CARIDI
PART II

INTO THE OBLIVION

THE 66TH REBIRTH OF FRANKIE CARIDI
PART II

BY JOHNNY MARCIANO

ILLUSTRATIONS BY ASHLEY MACKENZIE

Penguin Workshop

PENGUIN WORKSHOP
An imprint of Penguin Random House LLC
1745 Broadway, New York, New York 10019

First published in the United States of America by Penguin Workshop,
an imprint of Penguin Random House LLC, 2025

Text copyright © 2025 by John Bemelmans Marciano
Illustrations copyright © 2025 by Ashley Mackenzie

Penguin Random House values and supports copyright. Copyright fuels creativity, encourages diverse voices, promotes free speech, and creates a vibrant culture. Thank you for buying an authorized edition of this book and for complying with copyright laws by not reproducing, scanning, or distributing any part of it in any form without permission. You are supporting writers and allowing Penguin Random House to continue to publish books for every reader. Please note that no part of this book may be used or reproduced in any manner for the purpose of training artificial intelligence technologies or systems.

PENGUIN is a registered trademark and PENGUIN WORKSHOP is a trademark of Penguin Books Ltd, and the W colophon is a registered trademark of Penguin Random House LLC.

Visit us online at penguinrandomhouse.com.

Library of Congress Cataloging-in-Publication Data is available.

Printed in the United States of America

ISBN 9780593660973

1st Printing

LSCC

Design by Jay Emmanuel

This book is a work of fiction. Any references to historical events, real people, or real places are used fictitiously. Other names, characters, places, and events are products of the author's imagination, and any resemblance to actual events or places or persons, living or dead, is entirely coincidental.

The authorized representative in the EU for product safety and compliance is Penguin Random House Ireland, Morrison Chambers, 32 Nassau Street, Dublin D02 YH68, Ireland, https://eu-contact.penguin.ie.

PROLOGUE

Right now, Frances Caridi is walking on water.

"Brava!" Natas calls out after her with a single clap of the hands. Sitting on the grassy bank beside him, Wilma bares her fang-like teeth in an approving smile.

Walking on water. How it bothers Silvenus, this silly sort of spectacle in which Natas loves to indulge himself. Naturally, Frances loves it, too. What fourteen-year-old wouldn't? She's proud of herself, so proud that it makes the old satyr feel small for being such a grouch.

He should just enjoy this splendid June day, watching the late afternoon sun sparkle off the surface of the lake. Oh, how he loved to come here once upon a time. What glorious Saturday picnics they would have on the grand old dock. And the Boathouse! It's hard to believe that the godforsaken pile of stones and rubble on the far shore was formerly the site of such joy and camaraderie. Why doesn't Natas have it rebuilt?

Meanwhile, Frances, walking on water. Or rather, standing.

"What's wrong?" Natas hollers.

"Why don't I fall in when I stop?" Frances calls back, hands on hips. "Are you giving me some kind of boost?"

"Being as*sisted* is not cheating," Natas shouts. "The power of the Oblivion is itself a 'boost.' I am merely adding to it."

"It's a little bit cheating," Wilma says.

Frances insists on Natas removing his telekinetic support. With a shrug, he does.

She plunges in.

Silvenus laughs—he can't help it. But something is wrong. The girl is flailing about in panic.

"She doesn't know how to swim!" Wilma says.

Natas lifts the girl back out by way of his mental powers, apologizing profusely, while Wilma rushes into the lake, so panicked herself one might think it was she to almost drown.

"I'm okay, Wilma," Frances tells her.

"Take her back to your room," Natas says, putting a hand on Wilma's shoulder. "You should be getting ready for your flight, anyway."

As he and the old satyr watch the girls follow the path back to Croton, Natas says, "She always knows how to swim." He shakes his head. "It is one of the first things the girl should remember."

"She has hardly progressed since the fall," Silvenus says. "If anything, Frances seems to be *re*gressing."

"When they arrive for the summer retreat, the Listeners expect to welcome back Mother," Natas says.

"Perhaps you shouldn't have promised them that."

Natas shrugs. He doesn't actually care about disappointing the Listeners.

"They have been waiting sixteen years, what does one more matter?" Natas says. "Besides, they will still believe they are witnessing a miracle."

A miracle, or a typical example of the American teen on the precipice of high school? Because, outside of her ability to channel the Oblivion, this is precisely what young Frances is. Of course, even without her memories, she is very much herself. More so than in past lives.

"And who knows?" Natas continues. "Perhaps being in the company of so many old friends will jolt her memory."

A nice thought. In truth, the old satyr is more disappointed than Natas at Frances's failure to recall who she is. And yet, a part of him hopes that she never does, for her sake.

For his own sake, well, it will be most lonely if she doesn't.

PART ONE

RETREAT

1

Big News

Brand New Sign
Same Loving God

"Hey, look at that sign! It's clever."

"Yeah, Ron," Frankie says, "we know about the signs."

Ron—that's Mom's boyfriend.

How much does Mom like Ron? Enough to make Lucie sit in the back seat of the Prius with Frankie. That's a first.

"I thought Lucie needed the extra hornroom," Frankie says, smirking at her little brother. He's not amused.

"But Ron is so tall!" Mom says.

Ron is so not. Still, Frankie is happy that her mother is happy, especially since it makes Mom nice to her. Also a first.

At the Wagon Wheel, Ron attempts to take charge, saying in his man voice, "Four for lunch," having no idea who the girl working the register is.

Sylvie shoots a *who-is-this-guy?* look to Frankie as she gets up from behind the counter to hug Mom. She's one of those good parent friends who looks an adult in the eye and asks how they're doing and stuff.

"I love your new hair," Mom says.

Such a lie, because there's no way Mom likes her buzz cut. Sylvie runs her hand over her stubbly head and thanks her. "How'd graduation go?"

"Ek was amazing!" Lucie says.

"His speech was *wonderful*," Mom says. "You should've seen how proud his parents were."

At the booth, Ron uses his iPhone to magnify the menu and makes a dad joke about the funny-sounding platter names that's too lame to put in print.

"Who's the *freak*?"

Dink comes over to their table in his *Land of the Free, Home of the Awesome* T-shirt.

"The 1990s called," Lucie says. "They want their mullet back."

Ron looks alarmed, wondering if he's going to need to defend Lucie's honor. Even after they fist-bump each other, Ron's still confused.

"They're cool," Frankie says. "I mean, they're so *not* cool, but they're friends."

Ron fake laughs and Mom gives him a kiss. It still weirds out Frankie to see her mother all affectionate with some guy. Or to have a friend. The only person she ever talked to before was Uncle Sal.

"A number three, a number eight, and two number elevens," Mistral says, serving the dishes. He almost bashes Frankie in the head with one of his long pointy horns as he puts her plate down.

"I can't believe you're working here," she says.

"And I can't believe I'm staying in Dink's dead grandmother's room," Mistral says. "When do you guys start your jobs at the Institute?"

"Orientation's tomorrow," Lucie says, smothering his veggie scramble in hot sauce.

Giving up meat hasn't been easy for Lucie. His eyes follow

every movement of Ron's sausage links from plate to mouth. Just as longingly, Frankie watches Mistral and Sylvie laugh as they clear off the counter. Working at the Wheel seems way more fun than being a counselor at a summer retreat for old people.

"We have big news," Mom suddenly announces. She grabs Ron's hand.

Frankie freezes, fork suspended in front of her open mouth. *Mom and Ron are having a baby—and they're turning my room into the nursery.*

"Ron's moving in with me. We're going to live together!"

Relieved, Frankie exhales and takes her bite of food. "Don't you guys, like, already live together?" she says, chewing.

"We're ready to fully 'blend,'" Ron says, like they're a smoothie. "Besides, with both of my kiddos off to college, the old house is too darn big. I put it on the market last week."

"He's already got two offers," Mom says.

"Hey—Big Bow Hunter!" Ron says, pointing to the corner by the bathrooms. He wipes his mouth and gets up from the booth. "I used to love that game. Come on, Rose, let's play."

Frankie laughs at the thought of Mom playing a video game. But there she is, picking up the plastic crossbow.

"They grow up so fast, don't they?"

Ignoring Frankie's comment, Lucie gets all serious. "Isn't this a little quick? Ron's great, but they only met six months ago. Online."

"How else do old people meet?" Frankie says, drinking some water. "Time's running out for those two."

2

The Counselors

Campus feels eerily quiet, almost abandoned. On a nice day like today, the steps up the hill are usually packed with kids hanging out. Today, there's one lone tabby cat sunning himself. Or Frankie thought there was; as they walk closer, the cat turns out to be a notebook someone left.

Weird.

"So what do you guys think this is gonna be like?" Moira asks.

"I don't know, but I can't wait to find out!" Lucie says, as if they're about to skateboard down a rainbow.

"I'm scared!" Moira says for no other reason than to grab Lucie's arm.

It's disgusting.

Moira is a Scottish norm with long orange braids who's a year ahead of Frankie at school. Last night playing cards in the dorm was the first time Frankie ever hung out with her, and they didn't exactly bond. Moira is either the worst card player ever or she was purposefully losing. All she cared about was getting Lucie and Oxnard's attention. Ox, who's now talking. About what, Frankie couldn't care less. The oversize, handlebar-horned, I'm-him, Australian rugby bro is her least favorite kid on campus, and quite possibly the planet.

Inside the Mothership, the four of them give a quick bow to the portraits of Mother and the Founder and head up the stairs. The old mansion is practically a greenhouse, and it feels like they're climbing the degrees of a thermometer as they walk up the stairs to Dr. Natas's apartment.

Inside, the other two are already there. Lucie gives Ek a bro hug but he's not quite sure how to greet Efrat. "So you're a counselor, too, huh?"

"Why else would I be here?" Efrat says, like it's the dumbest question ever asked.

Efrat might be the only person at school not charmed by Lucie. As much as Frankie likes that about her, she's otherwise totally intimidated by the Israeli deem. She's going to be a senior but looks like she's in college, and is almost as tall as Ox. Other deems with pointy ears hide them, but Efrat tucks her black hair behind hers to show off how long they are.

"We have all arrived, I see, and on time no less," Dr. Natas says, coming out of the kitchen carrying a silver tray. "A fine beginning."

Dr. Natas places the tray down on the dining table and invites the kids to sit and take a cup of tea. Holding one under her nose, Frankie inhales the deep aroma of fresh hay. She used to not drink Dr. Natas's tea because she was suspicious of it—suspicious of everything—but now she gulps it down.

"Before we start, I must remind you of one thing," the head of school says. "Everything we do—all that we practice and teach over the next six weeks—must only ever be discussed among the persons in this room."

"What happens at the cult stays at the cult!" Ox looks around to see who laughs, but not even Moira is smiling. You don't make jokes around Dr. Natas.

The principal glowers at Oxnard, then continues.

"I dislike asking you to keep secrets from your parents. After all, should knowledge not be free and open to all?" Dr. Natas asks rhetorically. "In an ideal world, absolutely. In the real one, however, certain knowledge can be dangerous, and—in the wrong hands—cata*strophic*."

Frankie is pretty sure he's talking about the gym sisters.

"With that bit of business out of the way," Dr. Natas says, "I give the floor over to our senior counselors to explain what is expected of you over the coming days and weeks."

Ek gets up and smiles like he did for every award he won at graduation. This is his fifth time as a counselor, he tells them, and Efrat's second. "And I'm sure Efrat will agree that our number-one job is making sure that the Listeners have a fantastic Pythagorean Institute experience."

"What's a 'Listener'?" Moira asks.

"Awesome question!" Ek says, even though it's not. At the info session in the spring, Dr. Natas explained that *Listener* was what the Founder called his followers, back when the Institute wasn't a school but a year-round cult of flying yogis.

Efrat says that this year's attendees include four Listeners from back in the day; the rest are younger. "One is coming for her fourth retreat, and two are new this year."

"And of course there's Wilma!" Ek says. "She grew up spending summers here with her grandpa, who's a super-amazing man. But *you* must know all about him, right, Frankie?"

Being Wilma's roommate, you'd think Frankie did, but Wilma hasn't said one word about him, no matter how many times Frankie's asked. Of course, that's Wilma. Thumbs-up emoji aside, she hasn't responded to a single text Frankie's sent since leaving for Arizona.

Efrat and Ek go over what they'll be doing for the next week to get the place ready for the Listeners' arrival and what the daily schedule of the retreat will be.

"Tai chi, meditation, spinning, and weaving," Ek says, listing some of the activities. "You'll participate in all the same things the Listeners do, except when they go behind the veil."

"What happens behind the veil?" Ox asks.

"That is not for you to know," Efrat says.

"We do get to fly, though, right?" Moira asks.

Ek and Efrat look to Dr. Natas. He smiles.

"That depends on you. All of you," Dr. Natas says, turning from Moira to the rest of the counselors. "What is more important than flying, however, is that the six of you learn to channel to-*gether*, an experience that will teach you that even the most interior of journeys is best traveled with companions." He turns back to Moira with a smirk. "And, yes, you shall fly."

Even though she's snapping along with the rest of the counselors, Frankie groans inside. It's still hard for her to get over not being the only kid on campus who can channel.

"Any other questions?" Dr. Natas asks.

Ox raises his hand.

"When do we get paid?"

Dr. Natas lifts an eyebrow and smiles. "Saturday mornings," he says. "Until tomorrow, counselors."

3
Housekeeping

The dog barks, circling the back half of the flock, goading the sheep into the pen. He's seriously enjoying himself.

"As you can see, Argus does most of the work of herding," Mr. Silvenus tells the counselors. "Beyond feeding and watering, your job is counting. If there are fewer than forty-four sheep, you need to search the fields for strays. If there are more—well, you need to practice your math."

From a distance, the sheep look like big fluffy clouds, but up close, you can see their wool is yellow and burrs and thorny branches are stuck to their fleeces. And you seriously don't want to look at their butts.

"They need a haircut," Moira says. "And, like, a shampoo."

"A good shearing is what they need, which you and the Listeners will provide next week," Mr. Silvenus says. "These sheep play a vital role in our retreat. What once was grass and today is wool will in six weeks' time be transformed into something else entirely." The Latin teacher claps his hands. "I can hardly wait!"

From the sheepfold, they walk to the Mothership. At the closet under the back stairs, Mr. Silvenus hands out supplies and cleaning assignments. After sending the others upstairs, Mr. Silvenus leads Frankie and Efrat to the apartment they'll be cleaning, just down the hall from the closet. During the school year, Mr. Amadou and his family live here; for the retreat, it'll be home to Wilma and her grandfather.

"To avoid stairs," Silvenus says, explaining why they're getting put on the ground floor. "Poor Cadmus has become rather frail, I'm afraid."

"Cadmus?" Frankie asks. "That's his name?"

"It's the nickname Mother gave him. Which is only fair, as he's the reason for her being called *Mother*," Mr. Silvenus says. "Cadmus grew up at the Institute after his birth mother abandoned him here."

"His mom just left him?"

"The 1950s were a different time," the Latin teacher says. "She had come here looking for answers, but didn't find any she liked."

As Mr. Silvenus leaves, Efrat plugs in the vacuum cleaner. "Did you get to know Cadmus last summer?" Frankie asks. "What's he—"

The blast of Efrat starting the vacuum drowns out the rest of Frankie's question.

"SCRUB THE BATHROOM!" Efrat says over the noise.

The bathroom isn't anywhere near as gross as the ones at the gym, but it feels super weird for Frankie to be cleaning her history teacher's toilet.

"You call *this* clean?" Efrat points at the black mildew on the grout between shower tiles. "This should be white."

With anyone else, Frankie would say something snarky, but she's completely cowed by Efrat. It's not just how tall and beautiful she is, but the way she states things. Like she's infinitely right, and you're unbearably stupid.

"Not like *that*," Efrat says when they're making the bed. She comes to Frankie's corner of the mattress and takes the edge of the sheet away from her. "Like this. No wrinkles. Do that corner."

Frankie does as she's told. When she leans over to tuck in the sheet, the tiger's-eye amulet falls out from Frankie's T-shirt. Before she can stuff it back inside, Efrat presses her finger against it, pinning the amulet to Frankie's chest.

"This necklace—it's the one in Mother's portrait," she says. "Why do *you* have it?"

Face burning, Frankie can't think of an answer. She keeps it hidden precisely so no one asks her about it.

"Why are you embarrassed?" Efrat says. "I don't care. I just want to know the reason."

"I, uh, found it."

"Finders keepers?" The phrase sounds totally wrong with Efrat's accent. "I assumed it was because you have such strong abilities. Like Mother did."

Efrat starts to put the pillowcases on.

"Don't be embarrassed by being good at something," she says. "The only reason I'm here is to improve my skills."

The pillows done, Efrat looks at the bed, dissatisfied. There are diagonal creases in the top sheet, and bunching at the corners. Then, the wrinkles start to vanish and the folds grow tighter until the sheet is stretched across the mattress like a balloon about to burst.

"The powers *are* useful."

Frankie gets a little sick, seeing how good Efrat is.

When Dr. Natas told her that other kids had been learning how to channel in secret, Frankie was shocked.

"Come now, Frances," Dr. Natas said. "Surely you did not imagine yourself to be the only child I was training."

She definitely did. Wilma had been showing Frankie how to levitate, but said her grandpa taught her. Frankie only found out about the other kids when Dr. Natas took on Lucie as a student. It gutted her, and still does, because channeling is *her* thing, and what if Lucie is better at it than her? Her brother's refused to show Frankie what he can do, saying he's not any good, but Lucie is so humble, it only makes her suspicious.

The worst thing, however, would be if Ox is better than her.

4

Om

All the desks and chairs from the biology classroom have been pulled into the hallway, except for the heavy metal desk up front where Dr. Natas is standing.

During the school year, the only class Dr. Natas teaches is meditation, but today he's leading a session in channeling.

"If the notion of meeting in a science classroom seems ironic to any of you, rest assured that it is not. For what we shall study here is not magic but the physics of mind over matter: teleki*nesis*. Now," he says, holding up a pencil, "let me see what each of you can do with this." The principal places the pencil on the desk with a plink.

Lucie goes first, and any fear that he's being humble about his channeling skills vanishes. He struggles to even raise the pencil, which wobbles and shakes for so long before lifting off the desk that Frankie feels bad for her little brother. She feels great, however, to see that Ox is every bit as remedial as Lucie. Moira's even worse. All she can do is get the pencil to roll.

"Very good," Dr. Natas says encouragingly.

Ek is definitely not remedial. He lifts a sharpener as well as the pencil, sticking the one inside the other and spinning them in opposite directions while directing the peeled curls into the trash. It's seriously impressive.

Mr. Natas plucks the pencil out of the air. "Very sharp," he says, pricking his thumb with the tip.

Efrat does Ek one better, using the pencil and a piece of paper to write a poem—in cursive. Frankie can't even *read* cursive.

Topping that seems impossible. Thankfully, she doesn't have to try. "I believe we have all previously seen what Frances can do," Dr. Natas says. "So let us now move on to levitation."

Dr. Natas says it as matter-of-factly as Ms. Jenkins tells them to go get their microscopes, but how can it be so simple? Levitation is way more difficult than animating writing implements. When Wilma started teaching her, Frankie just bounced around on her butt. It took her a month to get airborne, and even now the highest she's ever made it is onto the bed. Maybe Ek and Efrat can do it, but the other three? No way.

The same as in meditation class, Dr. Natas invites them to sit in a circle on the floor and says, "Let us commence with the sacred sound of Om."

The first time Dr. Natas started going *ohmmm* in class, Frankie burst out laughing. *Like, seriously?* But now it's one of her favorite things, the way you feel the vibration of everyone humming inside your chest, in your bones even.

Chanting done, Dr. Natas has them do a breathing exercise, and then leads them through a body scan.

"To levitate a pencil, one applies their inner force to an external object," he says. "The levitation of one's own self instead requires the internal process of allowing. You al*low* the air around you to become heavier than your body; you al*low* yourself to rise."

It's like what Wilma has been telling her, except what took Wilma six months to get across, Dr. Natas says in six seconds. Still, Frankie doesn't see how this will get Lucie and the others off the ground, except they're already off the ground. And so is Frankie.

How did this happen? She's not even trying! This isn't like the hidden boost Dr. Natas gave Frankie to help her walk on water; it's like wearing floaties in a pool. Frankie couldn't stay down if she tried.

Without having to concentrate so hard, Frankie can enjoy the pure bliss of the ride they're all on—until she hears the sound of vomiting. And feels a splatter on her face.

Gross!

Even though they're only a foot or two off of it, the kids come clumsily crashing down to the floor. On their sides, they burst into uncontrollable laughter. Not because someone threw up—because what they just did was so crazy fun.

The only one not laughing is the vomiter.

"It is entirely normal," Dr. Natas says, comforting Moira. "For some, the first journey into levitation brings on a sort of seasickness."

"Dude, did you *feel* that?" Lucie says to Ox after handing Moira a paper towel.

"Mate—we were *flying*!"

The two of them do their bang-horns thing as Efrat says, "That was far from flying."

It *was* insanely cool, however.

5
Cryptic

Omnia mutantur nihil interit: "Everything changes, nothing dies."

At lunch, kids joke that the words on the ceiling of Chapel should be "The menu changes, the smell never dies." The summer heat makes it worse, releasing the odor of years of curry vegetable stews, fake chicken nuggets, and every form of cabbage known to humanity. Thinking that scrubbing the kitchen would be less disgusting than scooping manure out of the sheepfold with Efrat and the boys might've been a miscalculation. Frankie's glad when Ek has them take a break to fold up the cafeteria bench tables. In their place, they pull three wooden tables out of the storeroom, placing them end to end.

"The group dinners are my favorite part of the retreat. The stories the Listeners have!" Ek says, spreading out a long tablecloth. "I'm going to miss this cafeteria."

"Are you sad to be leaving?" Moira asks, starting to bring the chairs.

"I'm not completely leaving."

"Tokyo is pretty far from Proserpina, PA," Frankie says.

"But I'll be staying in the Pythagorean Institute family!" Ek says.

Ek is spending the next year helping Dr. Natas set up the "Ring of Inspire." Cringiest name ever.

"I can't believe you're deferring Yale," Frankie says.

"To be on the ground floor of a non-profit that's going to provide relief to disaster survivors all over Asia?" Ek says. "That was an easy decision!"

Ek is the kind of person who makes you feel guilty just by existing. Can he possibly be this good of a human being?

"Aren't you afraid of the earthquakes and volcanoes and stuff?" Moira asks.

Ek waves off the worry. "Our aim is to provide long-term support after the danger has passed. We're not going to be one of these organizations that forgets about the people we're helping as soon as the next disaster hits. But enough about me!" Ek says. "Time for the chafing dishes."

"That's such a gross word for something you put food in," Frankie says.

"They keep it warm!" Ek says.

Ek might be the best person ever, but he has zero sense of humor.

Walking down to the basement, Ek explains that the meals for the retreat get prepared off campus. "Bob picks up the food trays with the van, and it's our job to heat them up with sternos, which you can grab in the closet."

Frankie tries the door. "It's locked."

"Not that one," Ek says. "That goes into the crypt."

"The crypt?" Frankie says.

"This *was* a chapel," Ek says. "The crypt is where they keep the bones."

"Of *humans*?" Moira says.

Ek nods, like having a cemetery under the cafeteria is the most normal thing in the world.

"Whose bones are they?" Frankie asks.

"People from back in the sanatorium days," Ek says. "And the Founder and Mother, of course."

"From the portraits?" Moira asks.

"They're the only Founder and Mother I know!"

Frankie lingers at the door. It smells creepy in there. Can something *smell* creepy?

6

Jaguar

Enclosing the gravel courtyard behind the Mothership is a long garage faced with heavy wooden doors. At the side entrance, Mr. Silvenus peels up one corner of a mossy welcome mat to pick up a key.

"Nice security system," Frankie says.

"It's worked for forty years," Mr. Silvenus says, turning the lock and opening the door. "Mostly."

From the inside, he unbolts the middle set of doors and swings them out to make his big reveal.

"Whoa, what is *that*?" Lucie asks.

"A 1961 Jaguar roadster, the first year of the E-type," Mr. Silvenus proudly says as he gets into the driver's seat. "This fine chariot once belonged to the Founder. That man loved sports cars even more than he did expanding the mind."

Like any good cult leader.

The tailpipe coughs out smoke as the Latin teacher backs the pale-blue convertible out of the garage and over to the water hydrant.

Mr. Silvenus tells Ek and Efrat to take out the van and golf cart, too. "We'll be washing all three of them today," he says. "Or, should I say, *you* will."

"Don't they have car washes in Pennsylvania?" Frankie says, lying on the gravel trying to get the caked-on mud off the rear bumper of the van. She can't reach the bucket, so she channels the sponge over to the sudsy water and wrings it out with her mind. Which gives her an idea.

"Are you *crazy*?!" Lucie yells, twisting to get the sponge out from under the back of his shirt. "Why did you *do* that?"

"Because I can," Frankie says. "If you practice hard enough, you can do it, too, little bro. Just like Dr. Natas has been saying."

Of course, Lucie doesn't need channeling skills to turn on the hose. It's *freezing*. Frankie scrambles out from under the van and runs away. The situation devolves into a free-for-all, with Ox throwing a bucket of soapy water at Moira and even Ek and Efrat going at it.

"You're supposed to be washing the vehicles, not each other," Mr. Silvenus says, returning.

"But we're done," Ox says. Which is almost true.

"Excellent. Now you may start waxing the Jaguar," Mr. Silvenus says to Efrat and Ek. "In the meantime, I will teach our new counselors how to operate the golf cart."

Gathering the four of them together, Mr. Silvenus goes over the basics: the on/off switch; gas pedal; brake; and parking brake. Then the ground rules.

"This vehicle is *only* to be used to help shuttle the more aged of the Listeners around campus," he says. "As well as myself, of course. Now, who would like the first lesson?"

Four hands raise. Moira does that "Ooh! Ooh!" thing like she's in second grade.

Frankie's turn comes last. Once she gets in on the driver's side, Mr. Silvenus tells her to disengage the emergency brake—in Latin.

"No fair," she says. "School's over."

"I thought you might miss the sound," Mr. Silvenus says as Frankie presses on the gas pedal.

The golf cart goes way faster than you'd think, and it's not that hard to learn to drive, either.

"No one said it was." Mr. Silvenus smiles.

Could driving a car be anywhere near this easy? Sylvie got her permit three weeks ago; Frankie can't believe she still has to wait two more years.

The Latin teacher has Frankie drive to the front gate and turn around. Coming back toward the garages, Frankie is bummed her turn is about to be over. So is Mr. Silvenus, apparently.

"Why don't you turn toward the lake?"

Other than directions, the Latin teacher doesn't say a word, which is so not like him. Mr. Silvenus can't stand a silence. Even during tests, he talks the whole time. It's part of what makes him such a great teacher. Also his being prepared.

At the end of the school year, most teachers are so far behind that they rush through the material and you wind up learning nothing. Not Mr. Silvenus. He left extra time for the final assignment, which tied together their entire year of translating the *Metamorphoses*.

His final lecture was held inside Chapel. Why, Frankie had no clue, until Mr. Silvenus told them to open their copies of Ovid to the final book, line 165. It read: *Omnia mutantur nihil interit.* The same words as on the ceiling.

"The speech of Pythagoras," Mr. Silvenus said, "is *the* most important passage in the *Metamorphoses*."

Unlike the gods and semi-mythical heroes from earlier stories, Pythagoras was a real-life guy, and while he might be famous for triangles, as a philosopher he was way more into reincarnation.

"*Everything changes, nothing dies* sums up the essential belief not only of Pythagoras but I daresay of Ovid himself," Mr. Silvenus said. "These four simple words mean that we—both humans and animals—exist in a constant state of death and rebirth. Not only is our station in life never fixed, but our *species* changes from life to life."

Mr. Silvenus talked so long that day that Frankie missed half of her next class. And now, not talking, even though Frankie is stopped where the road Ts into the eastern wall, waiting for him to say which way—right back to school, or left into the woods.

"Are you okay, Mr. S.?"

He blinks once and looks around like he forgot where he was. "Oh, I'm fine. Just a tad . . ." He pauses. "Apprehensive."

"Why?" Frankie asks.

"Seeing the Listeners again. Particularly Cadmus. He was a vital figure at the Institute for a very long time, and such a vigorous person. But the last time I saw him—when he dropped off Wilma in the fall—the man could barely walk." Mr. Silvenus shakes his head. "Humans are so poorly constructed."

Seeing the concern on Frankie's face, he pats her arm and

says, "I am also positively joyous at the thought of seeing my old friends again. 'Old' being the operative term." He smiles.

"*Dextrum* or *sinistrum*?" Frankie says, making her Latin teacher smile even more.

"*Sinistrum,*" he says. "I am not quite ready to return."

7
Ritual

It's so hot that her shorts are almost dry, even though they just left the lake. The other kids swam and played Marco Polo; Frankie waded in up to her waist.

Not that she cared about getting left out of the game. She loved just being in the water. Of course, she's loved everything about the day off. From waking up late to getting her first paycheck to the milkshake at Jimmy Sprinklez to the epic game of tag they had in the woods right before jumping in the water, it's all been fun.

For Frankie, this is new. Not only has she never had a summer job before, she's never enjoyed summer. She hates the beach—she's pretty sure she's allergic to sand—and hates camps more. She used to hate just going outside; too sweaty, especially in her hoodie, baggy jeans, and Docs. Now she's wearing a T-shirt, shorts, and flip-flops, and she's got a tan for the first time since she was eight.

Who am I?

Frankie just hopes things don't change too much when the Listeners arrive tomorrow.

"Who's up for a game of hearts?" Ek says as they get close to the dorm.

Frankie wants to, but she's got to feed the sheep first—it's her turn on the schedule.

"I'll come!" Moira says.

"You don't have to," Frankie says. Meaning: *Please don't.*

Moira is always trying to get Frankie alone. She keeps talking about how we girls need to stick together, which is so not Frankie. It's not true, either. The reason Moira wants to hang out with Frankie is so she can talk about the gross crush she has on her little brother.

"Do you think Lucie likes me?" Moira says as they cross the meadow.

"I seriously have no idea."

The grossest part is the way she acts with him. She pulls the *I-hate-you* move with a grin, and the *you-make-me-so-mad* with a fake slap, which she must've learned from some YouTube flirting tutorial and which makes zero sense considering that Lucie has never made anyone mad *or* hate him. He just apologizes and looks confused.

"Your brother was *so* nice to me when I got sick."

"He got you a paper towel to wipe the throw-up off your face," Frankie says as she slides open the door of the sheepfold. "He did the same thing for Erol after he peed himself."

After filling the water buckets, they go into the feed room. When Moira hooks the top of the grain bin to the ceiling, her braids hit Frankie in the face. It's like an orange rope out to blind her.

"Can you *please*?"

The sheep hear the sound of feed being poured out and come

running, Argus barking after them. The flock clusters around the gate, pushing on it, while Frankie counts. The dog slips under the fence and circles Frankie, still barking. "You're supposed to herd *them*, Argus, not me."

She starts her count over and the dog nips her hand. "Stop it. You're messing me up."

But even after her third time counting she still gets forty-three. One sheep short.

"What's your count?" she asks Moira.

"Seventeen."

"Moira, that's not even close."

"It's too hard," she says. "They all look the same."

Frankie has no idea how they're going to find the stray, but Argus leads them right to it. The lost sheep is lying in a tall patch of grass in the middle of the meadow, its eyes glassy, its breathing labored.

"Is it okay?" Moira says as Frankie gets down next to the sheep.

It is so obviously not okay.

"We need to get Mr. Silvenus," Frankie says, petting the sheep's head. The poor thing looks scared and alone, its nostrils flaring. "One of us should stay here."

"You stay," Moira says, walking away.

Frankie doesn't want to be the one left alone, but Moira's already gone.

As she waits, Frankie looks into the animal's eyes and wonders what it's thinking. Could this sheep have been a person in a former life? According to Pythagoras, it definitely was, which is why he said that eating meat makes you a cannibal.

Do not exile kindred spirits
By wicked slaughter.
Do not let blood nourish blood!

Of course, Pythagoras also claimed to remember every single one of his past lives, a gift from his dad—Mercury. As in, the *god*. It turns out that Pythagoras was more of a cult leader than a philosopher, which makes him the perfect guy to name the school after. On so many levels.

Looking into the lonely, blinking eyes of this animal, Frankie is sure Pythagoras was right about one thing: We are all kindred spirits.

⁓

When the golf cart arrives, it's Dr. Natas instead of Moira who's riding next to Mr. Silvenus. Out in the field, kneeling over the sick animal, the head of school is clearly moved.

"Nothing can be done for this poor creature," he says sadly.

Standing there, an overwhelming déjà vu fills Frankie, the same kind that haunted her when she first got to school, that she never wanted to feel again. *Why is it back?* Frankie tries to ignore the feeling and concentrate on the present, on Dr. Natas stroking the sheep's soft muzzle, on the animal's flaring nostrils. Except, the nostrils no longer flare; in fact, it's not breathing at all. Or blinking.

The sheep is dead. How can it just be dead like that?

"Here?" Mr. Silvenus asks. With the tip of a shovel, the Latin teacher points to a spot on the ground a couple of feet away from the sheep.

Dr. Natas nods yes and walks to the golf cart, returning with two more shovels. He holds out one for Frankie.

"Digging is a true form of catharsis. From the Greek *katharsis*, meaning a purification, or cleansing," Mr. Silvenus says as their shovels slice through the roots of the grass. "We should all dig graves, not only for the animals who serve us but for our loved ones. Especially our loved ones."

"Aye," Natas says, flipping over a shovelful of dirt.

Frankie isn't sure if it's the shoveling or Mr. Silvenus's words, but the déjà vu returns even stronger, a vision of this exact act—the three of them, digging a grave.

Omnia mutantur nihil interit

Frankie uses the words from the ceiling of Chapel—from Pythagoras—as a mantra. Dr. Natas said that the words of a mantra don't matter, so choose ones you can remember.

Omnia mutantur nihil interit

Chanting a mantra helps calm the mind, he taught in class, and Frankie has been using hers to bury the visions when they overwhelm her. Instead of obsessing over her thoughts, she focuses on the sweat on her back, feels the wood of the shovel handle, smells the richness of the earth.

"I think I've had enough catharsis for the moment," Dr. Natas says, wiping the sweat from his forehead.

"Is it deep enough?" Frankie asks.

"Not quite," Mr. Silvenus says, handing her a bottle of water.

After taking a drink, she hands the water to Dr. Natas. They stand in silence, resting, until Frankie says, "Do you guys think reincarnation is real?"

The two of them look at each other like it's a crazy question, which Frankie supposes it is.

"Why do you ask?" Mr. Silvenus says, his furry eyebrows pressing down.

"I don't know." Frankie shrugs. "I keep thinking about Pythagoras. The *everything changes nothing dies* stuff."

"Ah," Mr. Silvenus says.

Dr. Natas begins to dig again. She expects the head of school to give one of his long, spiritualism-meets-science answers, but instead he just tosses aside a shovelful of dirt and says, "Yes, Frances. Reincarnation exists."

It's the answer Frankie was sort of hoping for, yet she finds herself nauseous, and worries that she's the one who's about to projectile vomit. Not because of Dr. Natas's answer; because of a realization.

The sheep didn't die on its own. Dr. Natas killed it.

She isn't sure if he strangled it with his mind or stopped its heart or what. He did it out of kindness, to stop its suffering, but still he killed it, and Frankie knows—somehow she *knows*—that he's done it before. And not just to sheep.

Blood pounds in Frankie's ear.

Omnia mutantur nihil interit

8

The Elephant in the Room

The old guy in the rainbow suspenders can't stop farting. Ox laughs every time.

"He can't help it," Ek whispers, hitting Ox. *"He's in his seventies!"*

"My granny is ninety and she doesn't walk around tooting a horn, mate," Ox says.

Moira laughs. And—as much as Frankie hates to admit it—so does she.

The man in the suspenders and white ponytail is a scrawny old hippie named Lonnie. He arrived with his wife, Diana, and their friend, Penny. Penny's face is deeply wrinkled except for around her wide, sharp cheekbones. Her mind, on the other hand, is anything but sharp. She just asked Frankie her name for the third time.

The counselors carry the Listeners' suitcases while Lonnie chats them up. Not seeming to hear her husband speaking, Diana loudly asks where Dr. Natas and Mr. Silvenus are. "And is Cadmus here yet?"

"Not yet, auntie." Ek calls them all *auntie* and *uncle*, his Nigerian accent coming out stronger when he does. "Dr. Natas and Mr. Silvenus should be bringing him and Wilma soon, though."

The rest of the attendees are already here. First came Eeva, who Efrat said is from Finland but seems American. She's as talkative as the three boomer hippies, but way younger and more of a pantsuit type. Eeva is a graduate of the Institute and was thrilled to get an apartment on the second floor. "Right next to my old room!" she said cheerily.

Up on the third floor are the ones Mr. Silvenus called "Dr. Natas's mystery guests." The mystery only got deeper when they arrived, as they barely talked and didn't want help with their bags. They didn't even give their names.

"Look at your ears!" Penny says to Efrat as she opens the

apartment door for them. "They get pointier every year."

Efrat smiles; it's the third time Penny has said this, too.

"My, what *lovely* flowers!" Diana says, delightedly smiling at the vase on the bedside table.

More farting. This time really loud.

"Maybe you should use the bathroom, dear," Diana says, her delight soured.

Lonnie turns to the kids.

"It's the elephant in the room!" he says, still farting. "There's no reason to pretend it isn't happening."

"I'm going downstairs to wait for the others," Diana says, annoyed.

"She doesn't like the sound of my chewing either. The romance is gone," Lonnie says after his wife leaves. "Lucky for her, she's going deaf."

Seemingly on their own, the clasps of Lonnie's suitcase unsnap and the drawers of the dresser open; folded clothes float from suitcase to drawer, with a pair of shirts continuing on into the closet where they slip onto hangers, the top button of each fastening.

Lonnie smiles at his accomplishment. "This is why I never miss cult reunion."

"I love this guy," Ox says as they leave.

How could you not?

The blue Jaguar shimmers so much from the wax that it looks like a chunk of sky is arriving to the front steps of the Mothership. Frankie leans against one of the stone griffins, excited to see Wilma.

Dr. Natas gets out of the driver's seat and pulls it forward, letting Mr. Silvenus and Wilma out of the back. While Mr. Silvenus and Dr. Natas go to the passenger's side to help lift Cadmus out of the bucket seat, Wilma opens the trunk, pulls out a walker, and sets it on the ground. Wilma's grandfather looks even weaker than Frankie expected and only seems stable once he's gripping onto his walker.

"He's the OG," Ek whispers to the younger counselors. "His first retreat was in the 1950s."

"Well, it looks like this is gonna be his last one, mate."

Efrat scolds Ox for the insensitive joke.

"There he is!" Lonnie says, exiting the Mothership.

"Cadmus!" Diana says, walking between her husband and Penny.

Diana gently squeezes Cadmus's arm and he lights up at the sight of the three of them.

Lonnie whistles. "This is the SUV of walkers you got here," he says. "I gotta get me one of these."

"Same old Lonnie," Cadmus says, shaking his head and smiling.

"And look how you've grown!" Diana says, turning to Wilma.

"Don't lie," Lonnie says. "Kids hate to hear lies. Wilma's the same size she was last year. The same height her mother was!"

"They *do* look alike," Diana says. "Your mother was such a dear soul . . ."

Hating the attention, Wilma mumbles something and looks to Frankie to come save her.

"So you're Frankie!" Cadmus says. "I've heard so much about you."

Before Frankie can reply, Dr. Natas says, "These two have had a long flight." He takes the bags out of Wilma's hands. "I shall bring them to their room."

Before she steps into the Mothership, Wilma leans into Frankie's ear. "If you thought things were freaky before," she whispers, "you haven't seen anything yet."

Fang smile.

9

Reckless

Dinner starts at five thirty and Mr. Silvenus is still organizing the seating at the long table inside Chapel, shuffling name cards from plate to plate. Having put himself in the middle across from Cadmus, he settles on placing Dr. Natas at the head of the table.

"Everyone wants to sit next to Dr. Natas, to drink from the fount of his wisdom," Mr. Silvenus says, his words dripping with sarcasm. "But they also want to be near Cadmus."

The Latin teacher has placed Cadmus between Wilma and Lonnie, with Frankie to Lonnie's left, at the end of the table with Diana and Penny. Why is she with the boomers? Frankie picks up her name card and asks if she can switch with the Finnish woman in order to sit next to Wilma.

"We can't have that," Silvenus says, pulling the card out of Frankie's hand and setting it back down where he had it. "Lonnie and the other two never sit with the newbies, as your generation calls them."

"We don't call anyone that."

Once the attendees arrive and get their food at the buffet, the table divides into several distinct conversations. On his end, Dr. Natas holds court with Eeva and his mystery Listeners, whom Frankie has found out are Brazilian (the woman) and Japanese (the man). In the middle, Cadmus holds court in a different way. He answers questions from Mr. Silvenus and Efrat, while Lonnie continues to tease him. Lonnie kids around with everyone, but with Cadmus it's like they're brothers.

Frankie sits next to Diana, who monologues to her, maybe because she can't really hear what anyone else is saying. This is fine by Frankie, who's learning all kinds of stuff, like how Cadmus is himself some kind of guru.

"Not a guru," Cadmus calls from down the table, his hearing way better than Diana's. "A simple yoga teacher."

"The teacher of teachers," Mr. Silvenus says to the counselors. "With a studio that still thrives."

"I hardly go anymore," Cadmus says, dismissing it.

"When are you going to retire?" Lonnie says.

"You never retire from the practice, you just *get* tired," Cadmus says with a smile.

Snapping quiets all the conversations as Dr. Natas stands to say how happy he is to have everyone here and what a splendid retreat they have in store.

"Before we embark on our shared journey, however, let us pause to remember those who no longer travel the path with us. This year we lost two of our fellow wayfarers. To Karl and Nasrat," Dr. Natas says, holding up a glass. "May we see you again soon."

"But not too soon!" Lonnie hollers. "Hear! Hear!"

"Hear! Hear!" everyone responds, glasses clinking.

That done, the old hippies talk about the lost Listeners. Karl's funeral was just last month.

"I was so sorry I couldn't go," Cadmus says.

"Well, Zurich isn't exactly around the corner from Arizona," Lonnie says. He leans forward, looking past Cadmus to Wilma. "You remember Karl, don't you?"

"Poor Wilma," Diana whispers to Frankie. "She was so young when her mother died. Breast cancer." She squeezes Frankie's hand. "Cadmus took her in—in his *seventies*. Of course, this was before he got sick. Such a shame."

"The first time Nasrat came to the Institute was a Tuesday, and it was raining," Penny says from across the table to no one in particular.

She can't remember two minutes ago, but the 1960s she remembers like they were yesterday.

After dessert, Dr. Natas excuses himself, and the two mystery Listeners leave with him. Instead of several fractured conversations, the table now has only one. Penny is nodding off, and even though it's only seven thirty, Frankie feels like doing the same as Lonnie and Cadmus go on about the picnics they used to have on the dock.

"There used to be a dock on the lake?" Lucie says.

"Oh, the widest dock you've ever seen! Beautiful!" Lonnie says. "And the Boathouse. On a summer evening like this, we'd sit inside and talk for hours, with the big sliding door open onto the water. I loved that building."

"It was glorious," Diana says. "And then Estelle and Mitzi did what they did."

"Mitzi was the one who did it," Lonnie says.

It takes a minute for Frankie to realize they're talking about the gym sisters.

"Remember how we drove down after the fire," Lonnie says. "How the building was still smoking?"

"Who cares about a building!" Penny says, suddenly awake and lucid. "The Founder died in that fire."

"Well . . . ," Lonnie says in a *that-goes-without-saying* voice.

"There was always something wrong with those two," Diana says, turning to Frankie. "Things were never the same after that fire."

Mr. Silvenus looks visibly uncomfortable with where the conversation is going, but it's Cadmus who speaks up.

"The Watson sisters didn't mean for the fire to happen," Cadmus says. "And this place changed well before the accident."

"What did he say?" Diana asks.

"That they didn't mean to do it!" Lonnie leans over and shouts.

Diana is flustered at having been corrected by Cadmus.

"But they were . . ." She searches for the right word. *"Reckless."*

"We all were." Cadmus smiles. "Still, I'm glad that you brought up those two, because it reminds me that I need to go say hello. They can get testy if you make them wait."

As Wilma gets Cadmus his walker, the old hippies look shamed by him, or maybe it's the situation.

"Frances," Cadmus says, turning to her. "Would you be so kind as to take me to the gym? I understand you have a . . . *special* relationship with the sisters Watson." Cadmus gives her a smile as he leans on the walker.

Following him to the door, Frankie shoots a *why-aren't-you-taking-him* look to Wilma over her shoulder.

Wilma mouths the words *really freaky* to Frankie and sits back down at the table.

10

Cadmus

The walk down the hill is taking way longer than usual, every step an effort for Cadmus. He and Frankie pass under the shadows of leaves, the setting sun visible from across the woods.

"The gym, we called it the spa, you know . . . That was before there was a school . . ."

Cadmus's conversation is halting from the effort of using his walker.

"In some ways, it had the same purpose . . . To improve your body." Cadmus smiles. "I think mine needs some improving, don't you?"

Frankie doesn't know what to say.

"Mother . . . ," Cadmus begins, but doesn't finish the thought. Then, "Mother first began to teach me—the channeling—when I was your age. In my mind . . . I'm *still* your age."

The path down becomes steeper, and Cadmus struggles to find solid ground for the walker. Frankie puts her arm on his back in a gesture of support.

Below, the gloomy stone gym building comes into view

through the tree trunks, reminding Frankie how disappointed Estelle will be that she's not bringing her any food. Yesterday was Saturday, the day Frankie usually stops at the O-K Kwik Mart, but with all the fun at the lake and stuff she didn't have time to go. Of course, Estelle will be nice about it; it's Not-Estelle that hates Frankie. Why, she still doesn't know.

"The sisters . . . ," Cadmus says. "It's the hardest time of year for them. They were members of our community. The others . . . shouldn't exclude them."

"I get why they're mad at the sisters, though. They did break the rules," Frankie says, parroting what Dr. Natas has told her. "They shouldn't have gone into the Oblivion." Saying the word *Oblivion* out loud sounds silly, but Cadmus doesn't blink.

"Seeking knowledge . . . There should never be a rule against that. Even if it has . . . consequences."

According to Dr. Natas, it wasn't knowledge the sisters were after, but she doesn't want to correct Cadmus.

"Lonnie and the others blame the sisters for . . . the death of the Founder. But Ramakrishna was an old man . . . already dying. He didn't have much time left. Like me." A fainter smile now. "But what they really blame the sisters for is the end of the good days . . . The end of the vital time of their lives."

With an audible exhale of relief, Cadmus stops to rest on the bench that overlooks the steeply wooded slope. Down below, the playing fields extend beyond the gym to the forest. Setting his walker off to the side, Cadmus removes his shoes and socks and rubs the soles of his feet, pulling them one at a time into a cross-legged seat. He then rests his hands on his knees, palms up, thumbs touching index fingers.

"You are very kind to walk an old man," he says, closing his eyes. "I can make it the rest of the way on my own."

"But how will you . . ."

Frankie doesn't finish what she was going to say because Cadmus has started meditating. A moment later, he levitates off the bench. Not a foot or two up like they've been doing in the biology room, but above Frankie's head.

Now, his entire body unfolds, and he isn't levitating, he's flying—actually flying. It's not super-hero flying, more that he glides across the air. Floating down the slope, the leaves in the treetops rustle as he brushes past them and, for a moment, the setting sun forms a halo around his body passing in front of it. Below, the glass doors of the gym breezeway open before him in a gesture of welcome.

Frankie has seen a lot in the past year, but nothing like this.

It's beautiful.

11

Monday

Tai chi is a slow-motion martial art, more experimental dance than exercise. Still, it's the perfect workout for the old hippies and totally hilarious to watch Lucie and Ox attempt, especially when Ox's long hooked right-side horn gets caught in one of Lucie's swirling ram horns.

"Hey, watch it!" Lucie says, falling off-balance.

After, Frankie argues with them over who gets to drive the golf cart. Pointlessly, as Mr. Silvenus picks Moira to take the Listeners to the sheepfold. The rest of the counselors walk.

"Perhaps no craft has been more significant than that of creating cloth out of animal fiber," Mr. Silvenus says, standing in the pen surrounded by six counselors, eight Listeners, and the now forty-three sheep. "As the days turn warm, we take our first step in warding off the inevitable chill of winter by relieving our four-legged companions of what has become an unpleasant burden." He holds up a pair of shears and snips at the air. "Their fleeces."

Mr. Silvenus gives a demonstration of how to shear a sheep, but it should've been Wilma—she's amazing with all cutting implements—or, even better, Lonnie. The scrawny old guy works incredibly fast, clipping one entire sheep in the time it takes others to do a small patch. The animal seems to sense he knows what he's doing, because it doesn't struggle when he puts it to its back to shear its belly. Frankie's sheep has less trust. It keeps trying to get up, and Frankie is worried she's going to stab the thing by mistake. Then she gets kicked in the shin. "Ow!"

The other counselors laugh, except—strangely—Ox.

"You have to hold 'em down firmly, mate," he says. "Let me have a go."

Being shown up by Wilma and Lonnie is one thing; being shown up by Oxnard is another.

"His parents own a sheep farm," Lucie says.

Frankie rolls up her pant leg to show the bruise on her shin.

"I don't see it."

"I'm *going* to have one—I can totally feel it." Frankie then scratches her itchy arms. "I think I'm allergic to wool."

Frankie knows how lame it is to complain, but she can't stop.

She's embarrassed by being bad, the same as Ox and Lucie were all last week during solo channeling, making excuses for why they couldn't pick up a hard-boiled egg or a walnut with their minds.

When it's her turn, Moira refuses to even try.

"The only thing left to do is its *butt*," she says, making a disgusted face at the almost bare sheep. "Do you see what's hanging off of it?"

"Dags," Ox says.

"What?"

"*Dags*. That's the Australian word for 'em."

"Australians have a word for *the poop that's stuck to the wool of a sheep's butt*?" Frankie says.

"There are a lot of sheep in Oz, mate."

⁂

The schedule posted on the front door of the Mothership is broken into color-coded blocks. There's green for the noon Lunch hour and a double block of blue for Free Time (read: nap). The yellow three to four p.m. rectangle is labeled Meditation but might better be marked Flying Yogi Time.

They do begin with a meditation, of course. The *ohm*ing sounds more powerful, not only because of the added Listeners, but because they're doing it in Chapel now; churches are made for chanting, after all. The vibration fills the space, reverberating off the high ceilings and stained glass windows. The sound tingles in their bones, and then their entire bodies start to hum.

Suddenly, they're off the ground. Not gently like before; this time they get jolted upward, and it's not like wearing a floatie. Frankie *is* the floatie, bobbing more violently the higher she gets pushed, starting to get the seasick thing. Once it's over, Frankie is relieved, even if standing on solid ground makes her feel heavy on her own legs.

"How was that for you, young fella?" Lonnie says, slapping Lucie on the back.

"*Way* more intense with you guys," Lucie says.

That's for sure.

Next on the schedule is Behind the Veil. "Why do they call it the *veil* if it happens in the basement?" Moira asks. Neither Ek nor Efrat knows.

Before going down to the crypt with the Listeners, Dr. Natas instructs the counselors on running their own channeling session. "The theme of week one is working together," he says. "Students learn most when they learn from each other. So go learn."

12

Pearls

A couple days in, the retreat has developed a rhythm. Tai chi is a nice way to start the day, and is surprisingly hard. Your arms get tired doing that slow-motion stuff.

Shearing has gotten super fun—Frankie and the sheep have come to an understanding—but she feels so sweaty and grimy afterward, she wishes she could take a shower. Instead, it's time to set up lunch. Frankie steals bites of curry as she lights the sternos, she's so freaking hungry.

At the table, Frankie understands why Mr. Silvenus stressed over who sits where. The three hippies really don't like the Mysterions, as Lonnie calls the two new Listeners. Not that the Mysterions are trying to be liked; they stick to each other when they're not sticking to Dr. Natas, and spend as much time in his office as they do participating in group activities.

The hippie Listeners also shun Eeva, who does make an effort and is here for the fourth time. Frankie gets the feeling it's less her being so much younger than the boomers and more her channeling abilities, or lack of them. The Finnish woman is as bad as Ox and Lucie. Having been a student at the Institute, Eeva gravitates toward the counselors, but she's old enough to be their mom. Frankie feels bad for her.

Today, Dr. Natas is introducing a new exercise: "the pearl." Everyone in the circle hovers just off the floor and concentrates on one person in the center—the pearl—lifting them all the way to the ceiling. The group then lets go, and the pearl must resist gravity on their own, the goal being to float to the ground as slowly and softly as possible.

The letting go isn't always for real, because half the counselors would break their necks without some help, and Eeva, too. (Cadmus, of course, doesn't even need help going up.) Frankie gets to be the pearl twice. The first time, she lasts all of three seconds—how fast she plummets is terrifying. On her next turn, she fights the fall long enough to earn snaps.

The most surprisingly good gravity defiers are the Mysterions; they might be new to the retreat but obviously not to channeling. Lonnie doesn't snap when they're done, he only gets more suspicious.

thought things would never be the same. And they're not. Frankie misses Sylvie not being at the Institute, but having a friend outside the walls is good, especially on a Saturday like today, since it gives her a place to get away from the other counselors, and the Listeners, too.

The Listeners. Frankie is bursting to tell Sylvie and Mistral about them. Last night, Dr. Natas hosted a dinner at his apartment to celebrate the end of the first week, and all kinds of details came spilling out.

"Do you guys remember Lonnie Appleseed?" Frankie says when the three of them are alone at the counter.

"You kidding?" Mistral says. "My aunt packed me one of those juice boxes every day."

"They came with an apple seed and instructions on how to plant it," Sylvie says. "I totally did that."

"*He's* the old guy with the rainbow suspenders and the ponytail. His wife and him still run the juice company."

Frankie couldn't believe it when Diana casually mentioned it.

"Wow, he must be rich!" Mistral says.

All the Listeners are successful. Like, crazy successful.

Penny was a model who acted in old horror movies; Cadmus had a line of how-to yoga videos back in the nineties; and Eeva used to be the *prime minister* of Finland.

"Wait," Sylvie says. "She *ran* the country? And she was a student at the Institute?"

"You know, we meet famous people here, too," Mistral says. "Andy at booth five was the eighth runner-up in the Nathan's Famous Hot Dog Eating Contest."

The Mysterions have also become less mysterious. "They

work at Sibylla," Lucie said. "It's an investment company Dr. Natas sits on the board of. They call him all the time."

As part of his after-school job, Lucie answered the phone in the principal's office.

"Why didn't you tell anyone you knew who they were?" Frankie asked.

Her brother shrugged. "No one asked."

"So is this like a corporate retreat for them?" Frankie said. "How did they learn to channel so well?"

Lucie doesn't know. "They don't exactly chat with me when they call."

Mistral is still talking about competitive eating when Sylvie's dad sticks his head out of the kitchen pass-through.

"Hey, I'm glad you guys are having fun, but I need you two in here to prep the dinner salads," he says to Sylvie and Mistral. "Javvy is still out sick."

"I should go anyway," Frankie says. Not that she wants to. Especially considering where she has to go next.

15

The Sisters

"Where were you last week?"

"I was busy with the retreat," Frankie says.

"Busy with *them*," Not-Estelle says. "Our former lifelong friends."

"Look, do you want this stuff or not?" Frankie says, holding up the snacks she brought from the O-K.

"We most certainly do!" Estelle says, snatching the plastic bag.

"Do you really think chips and soda will make us like you?" Not-Estelle says.

She's in an even worse mood than Frankie feared.

"We already like you, dear," Estelle says, waving Not-Estelle off with a Pringle. She bites into it. "And, sister, you're forgetting Cadmus. *He's* a lifelong friend."

"That's because Cadmus is a gentleman, and gentlemen don't forget." Not-Estelle reluctantly takes a chip. "I can only pray we outlive the rest of them. Two more died this year."

The thought cheers up Not-Estelle.

"But poor Cadmus! He looked so fragile," Estelle says. "What if he's next?"

"He'll definitely be next," Not-Estelle says, cheer gone.

Estelle sighs and takes a guzzle of Dr Pepper.

"Maybe I should get you guys fruit and, like, kombucha," Frankie says. "Or blueberries. They sell them at the farm stand on the way to town."

"Hmm," Estelle says, thinking. "How about a Milky Way?"

"You know this stuff is really bad for you," Frankie says.

"So you won't help us get out of this prison, but you're going to tell us what to eat?" Not-Estelle says.

"I don't have to buy you anything, you know."

A look of horror comes to Estelle. "Be quiet, sister!" Then to Frankie, "You only buy us these snacks once a week, dear. It's a treat!"

"I'd *rather* she help us escape," Not-Estelle says.

"How?" Frankie says. "There's no way Dr. Natas will ever lift the curse or whatever it is that keeps you guys trapped in here."

Frankie wants to ask why Mother put the hex on them in the first place. Cadmus planted a seed of doubt about whether they deserved it, and Frankie has never been clear on why they went inside the Oblivion in the first place. Dr. Natas said the sisters foolishly thought they could gain immortality, but could they have actually believed that?

In the end, Frankie doesn't ask them anything. She'd never get a real answer, and all it would do is lead to more complaining from Not-Estelle.

"You know what, dear? I think fresh blueberries sound splendid," Estelle says as Frankie leaves. "*And* a Milky Way."

16

Puzzles

"**Do you have** one with . . . ," Lucie says, pointing. "What do you call these things? The part that sticks out."

Lucie is holding up one of about a hundred pieces of blue sky. They're working on a vintage jigsaw puzzle they found at the bottom of the games closet. *The Great Wall of China*.

"That's the male," Ox says. "The holes are the female."

"You're disgusting," Frankie says.

"That's what they're called, mate."

"We always called them keys and locks," Lonnie says.

Lucie combs through the pile of sky that's been sorted out. "I think this puzzle is missing pieces."

The mere thought unravels Moira.

"Someone should count," she says.

"Go ahead," Frankie says. "It's only got a thousand pieces. And maybe less."

"Can *you* count?" Moira asks Ek.

For the first time ever, Frankie sees Ek shoot someone a dirty look.

"It is missing pieces," Wilma says, snapping a piece of wall into place. "I've done it three times before."

"Well, why didn't you bloody tell us?" Ox says, shoving the pieces away from him. "I hate puzzles anyway. Let's play spit."

There's no way Frankie is playing spit with Ox again. Last night he kept cheating and grabbing the smaller pile when she won.

"It's a game of speed, mate," he said.

"But what's the *point* of the game if anyone can grab the smaller pile?"

Frankie had wanted to kill Ox. She wonders how Dr. Natas avoids using his mind-murder trick on *everyone*.

"Should we get out of here?" Frankie says to Wilma.

Wilma stands up. "I need to get back to Grandpa, anyway."

The two of them walk across campus toward the Mothership. Shorn sheep graze the quad.

"They look naked," Wilma says.

"Maybe you should make them jumpsuits."

Wilma smirks. "Maybe I should."

They walk on in silence. It's weird—Frankie's been dying to

get Wilma alone, and now that she has, she can't think of anything to say. When they lived together, Frankie would just come home and tell her about whatever happened that day, it didn't matter if it was trapping a spirit or putting the decimal point in the wrong place on a math quiz.

"I miss us being in the same room," Frankie says.

"That's because I'm a great roommate," Wilma says.

Frankie also misses having someone around when she wakes up from the nightmares. Taking the amulet off didn't make the Mother dreams go away. What's worse, the other recurring nightmare is back, where everyone is talking Latin and the world is coming to an end and Mr. Silvenus has horns and keeps asking where her father is. She woke up last night with her sheets soaked in sweat. Frankie used to chalk it up to being a stress dream over her translation homework, but why is she having it in summer? And why is the nightmare so *real*?

"Well, see you in the morning," Wilma says when they get to her door.

It's all Frankie can do not to ask if she can stay over.

17

Dyed in the Wool

For week two, the morning activities get switched up, starting with yoga replacing tai chi. Frankie's psyched; she did yoga as her spring "sport" and can downward dog like crazy. But the best thing about Monday is getting to drive the golf cart.

"This is even more fun than levitation," she says, pressing the pedal to the floor as they close in on the sheepfold. She hits a rock in the field and Lucie knocks a horn into the roof support.

"Slow down!"

The siblings pull sacks of wool out of the feed room and load them onto the back of the golf cart, then return to the garages behind the Mothership. Efrat is filling a long galvanized metal tub with the hose to clean the wool in. It's a necessary step; the wool seriously stinks.

Unlike with the vehicles, this washing is pure drudgery, especially laying out the fibers to dry in the sun.

"Chin up! Tomorrow the true fun begins, when we commence the pigmentation process," Mr. Silvenus says. "Commonly, one waits for the wool to be spun into thread before dyeing. The colors have greater permanence, however, when the pigment is applied while the fiber is still loose, hence the term *dyed in the wool*."

The afternoon brings changes, too.

"The ultimate goal is that each and every one of us be able to levitate on our own," Dr. Natas says. "As a step forward, we will focus this week on practicing in pairs."

Frankie and Wilma aren't allowed to team up; instead, Frankie is put with Eeva. She still can't get over that this woman ran *Finland*. Hopefully, she was better at governing than she is levitating.

"I'm sorry!" she keeps saying.

"Never say you're sorry."

"I know, I know," Eeva says, flustered.

How can the former head of a country be so self-conscious?

When the Listeners go behind the veil, the counselors continue practicing, now with each other.

Frankie gets paired with Moira, who barely helps lift herself at all. Frankie has to levitate the both of them, which she can only manage for short bursts.

The whole experience is weirdly personal. Like holding hands, but with your mind, and Moira's is cold and clammy. Even after she rotates partners to Ek, the connection isn't broken; Frankie can locate Moira without looking. Not that she wants to.

Her next match is with Ox.

"Aw, shoot. Is that the Listeners I hear coming up out of the crypt?" Frankie says, cupping a hand behind her ear. "We must be out of time."

"No need convincing me, mate."

After dinner, Frankie lingers over rinsing the chafing dishes because she can't face going to sleep. It's like Mother herself is in that shoebox under the bed. You'd think having trapped actual ghosts would keep imaginary ones from haunting Frankie.

I can't be afraid to be in my own room, Frankie decides. So she goes there, gets the amulet, and walks back across campus to the Mothership. The lights are on in the top-floor dormer windows, so she knows he's awake.

"What is this about?" Dr. Natas says when he answers his door.

"Please, just take it," Frankie says, holding out the necklace.

Giving back a gift is bad manners and Frankie expects Dr. Natas to be disappointed, or even wounded, but he doesn't seem to be either.

"It is only a piece of jewelry, you know."

"But everyone thinks it's a piece of someone," Frankie says. "And I think they're right."

Natas accepts the amulet with a cryptic grin, closing his fist around it.

"Good night, Frances," he says, and shuts the door.

18
The Lake

Giving the amulet away worked surprisingly well. She's getting her second night of good sleep in a row. Then the knocking starts at—Frankie checks her phone—11:37 p.m.

"What is it?" she says, milking the hoarseness in her voice.

"We can't sleep!" Giggling outside her door. "It's too hot!"

"We're going to the lake!"

"SHH!"

"Don't wake Mr. S.!"

Whispering, then laughing.

"Bring your lighter," Lucie whispers.

"Ugh!" Frankie says. With no hope of getting back to sleep, she swings herself out of bed and joins the rest of the counselors.

Outside, they walk in the direction of the rising moon, one of those hugely full, bright orange ones that straddles the horizon and looks so close you feel like you could walk to it.

At the lake, Frankie stays in the shallow water like usual. Lucie keeps her company while the rest swim out.

"Marco!"

"Polo!"

Laughing.

Moonlight reflects off the lake in a trail leading to the ruins of the Boathouse. Under the water, mud oozes between her toes and feels so good that Frankie starts to squeeze her feet into it.

"Marco!"

"Polo!"

"Oh no!"

More laughing and splashing.

"Wanna build the fire now?" Lucie says.

Frankie thumbs her lighter. "Flame on."

As the siblings gather sticks and dried-out pine needles, Lucie keeps looking over to the moon, now up in the sky. Something dark passes in front of it. "Was that a bat?"

She doesn't think so, because it looks like—Frankie doesn't even want to *think* about what it looks like. Because how could it be what it looks like? She trapped all those. Even once they gather around the fire to tell scary stories, she keeps looking for more of them but doesn't see any.

The problem is, she *feels* them.

Omnia mutantur nihil interit

Ek tells a story that's not at all scary, then Efrat tells one that's positively terrifying, about a boy whose dead uncle lives in a trunk at the foot of his bed and comes out at night to talk to him.

"That's not real, is it?" Moira says.

"Of course it is," Efrat says.

Next, it's Ox's turn.

"I'm going to tell you a story that one of the Listeners told me while we were dyeing wool yesterday," Ox says, poking the fire with a stick. "It's something I've wondered about since I got to the Institute—what happened the night the Founder woke up in his bedroom to find the Boathouse in flames."

Ox points the glowing end of the stick in the direction of the ruins.

"The Founder lived on the second floor, with a window overlooking the lake. He was old and couldn't get himself out of bed anymore. Because of the cancer." Ox looks up at them, his face and horns reflecting the fire below. "The heat is what woke him up, and when he saw the flames, he cried out for help. Then a spark ignited his old horsehair mattress, and he started getting *burned alive*."

"Ox, really, I—"

Ox holds up a hand to stop Ek from interrupting. "Imagine what that bloody feels like, ay? What would you do? What could *he* do? The Founder must've had a rush of adrenaline, because he managed to use his channeling powers to lift a chair and smash the window. Then he half-levitated, half-jumped through the opening, plunging himself into the lake in hopes the water would put out the flames roasting his skin. But it was too late. *Shh!*" Ox puts a finger to his lips. "If you're quiet you can still hear his screams."

Moira's about to pee her pants, she's so terrified.

Ox drops the stick in the fire. "True story."

"It is so not true," Ek says. "The Founder never left his room. They found his blackened bones right in the ashes of his bed."

"That's even *freakier*," Moira says, hugging her knees.

Everyone laughs. "No one can top that," Lucie says, kicking dirt over the fire and stomping. The counselors head back toward the dorm together, still laughing. About what, Frankie is no longer sure.

Have you ever stopped to think, *This is the best moment of my life?* Or if not the best, then one you wouldn't trade for any other? Right now, Frankie is having one of those moments. A moment when she feels like everything she ever wanted is possible.

"Oh, shoot, guys," she says, stopping. "I forgot my lighter."

"I'll come with," Moira says, but Frankie won't let her. Because the lighter is right here in her pocket.

19
Sinking

The failure has been nagging at her ever since she fell in. It's not the humiliation—well, not only—it's that Frankie needs to prove to herself that she can walk on water without any boost. She's not wanting to fly like Cadmus, or levitate to the top of Chapel, or get airborne at all. Anyone can float on water; Frankie just needs to float on the soles of her feet.

Kicking off her flip-flops, she sits down cross-legged in the grass by the edge of the lake and levitates enough to hover her way over to the water. She skims the surface, her butt getting wet, and lets go little by little, allowing the water to carry her.

A breeze ripples the lake, and she bobs like a duck. More confident now, Frankie leans forward and places her palms down flat on the water to steady herself. She takes a deep breath and begins to crawl forward on her hands and knees. Hesitating, she starts to wobble and sink; she needs to keep moving to stay afloat. She crawls faster, now feeling solid, and swings her right leg so the sole of her foot is flat on the water, then her left, and she's standing, walking. Frankie is *walking*.

Walk as you have always walked. That's the advice Dr. Natas whispered in her ear when she walked over hot coals, and that's exactly what she's doing now. The water laps at her bare feet. It's so freaking *thrilling* Frankie doesn't want to stop. But where is she?

Looking around, she finds herself in the middle of the lake.

*The shore is **so** far.*

A waking vision possesses her, of being a hundred feet above the sea, desperately searching for land, but finding only water. *And I can't swim.*

Fear grips her body. Her confidence evaporates, and with it, the support of the water. In that instant, she plunges underwater.

Frankie begins to panic; Frankie begins to drown.

Under the surface of the lake, darker, wilder visions assail her. Of fire, of death—the Founder's death—and of a terrifying world of shadows. She remembers it all, racing through the flames, finding him, and entering the Oblivion, to bring them—the sisters—back inside the walls.

This is madness. Whatever's happening, she needs to shut it out, or she'll die.

Omnia mutantur nihil interit

The mantra calms her mind, and she feels herself again turn buoyant. Emerging to the surface, she breathes in sweet air, and, on instinct, begins to swim. But what instinct? How can she swim? The strokes flow—great, long strokes, like the strides of running. She remembers the joy so well, of swimming. Of swimming in this lake, and she makes for the shore of the ruined Boathouse like she once swam for the dock during Saturday picnic, when they—*we*—were the ones laughing.

Climbing out over the big rocks, breathing heavily, she thinks, *How do I remember those picnics?* She can see Lonnie, and Penny, and Cadmus, and they're so young.

She wants to remember nothing. She walks away from the lake in a fugue state, not aware of where she's going or what she's doing or who she even is until she finds herself in front of a door. Dr. Natas's door.

My door.

Frankie can't push away the truth she's been denying for so long. That you, reading this, have been waiting for. She knows where the memories are coming from—she knows who she is. Part of her did all along.

In the dream, when she gazed in the mirror, *her* face looked back. But it was no dream.

I'm Mother.

20

Go Insane

Frankie is in the supply closet under the back stairs, the one by the apartment where Wilma and Cadmus are staying. Chin on her knees, arms wrapped around her shins, she rocks back and forth, nauseous.

She needed to get away from the apartment but could barely

make it down the stairs, because those stairs! She stumbled on them once—it was in the nineties—and split open her forehead. Blood streamed down her face; she got twelve stitches.

She feels so stupid! The Listeners—they *know*, don't they?

"Mother, you **are** here."

That demented old woman said it! Penny. Frankie remembers the day she met her—that Mother met her—and how the girl wasn't wearing any shoes, how filthy her feet were, the disgust Mother felt. *These hippies.* Diana brought her to the Boathouse. Diana was just a girl then, too. They had a loaf of bread; they fed it to the swans.

The past is happening right in front of her.

In the closet, rocking back and forth. Violently.

Omnia mutantur

Maybe the memory is fake, Frankie thinks. Planted by a week of listening to stories of the old days.

But she can *hear* the music playing that day, *see* the portable stereo on the dock. It was blue—turquoise blue. She never liked this music, the Doors or the Rolling Stones or whoever it was.

nihil interit

The chanting works. For a moment. Then:

Reincarnation.

It **is** real. *How can it be real?*

Pythagoras! Huge flashing arrows have been pointing to the answer. This place is *called* the Pythagorean Institute, it's like they wanted her to figure it out.

Wait. Someone did want her to figure it out. *Mother* did.

Mother started the school; the *Metamorphoses* must be a message to herself. And the words on the ceiling—the words she's been chanting—*Everything changes, nothing dies!*

She's not just Mother, either. That weird ancient nightmare, when Mr. Silvenus is shaking her—she's that girl. And she's not even just *people*. The dream where she's a hawk, looking for land, that's no dream.

It's painful how much the keys and locks fit.

It's all true. She has to talk to Silvenus! He'll know. Because of Ovid. Because he was *in* her past lives.

She gets up to go to him but she can't go to him—not at two in the morning. Still, she has to go somewhere. Staying in this closet all night is not an option, and being alone isn't either.

"Wilma!"

Out in the hall, tapping on the door, whispering fiercely.

"Wilma!"

Wilma opens the door a crack, sleep in her eyes.

"Can I stay with you tonight?" Frankie says.

Wilma doesn't ask why, doesn't say a word. She just crawls back into bed and moves against the wall, to give her friend some room to get in.

21

The Scrutiny of Daylight

Sounds from the next bedroom of someone knocking around wake up Frankie. The first hint of dawn fills the lower part of the sky out the window, and she decides to leave before Cadmus comes in and she has to explain why she's here. Frankie gently removes herself from bed without waking Wilma and slowly opens and closes the door with the least noise possible.

Back in her own dorm, Frankie finds the moleskin notebook that Mom gave her for Christmas. She starts writing down her memories—to take control of them—but she doesn't get very far.

"Time to make the coffee, sis!"

Once it's ready, Frankie has the first cup.

"Good morning, Miss Caridi," Mr. Silvenus says, filling his mug.

Should she talk to him now? But how now, with other people here? And will he think she's lost her mind? Will he be right?

In the full light of day, Frankie starts to doubt the whole reincarnation thing. *I can't be Mother.* Let alone a bird. Somehow she gained these memories, like when the spirits flowed through her and she downloaded their lives. Could Mother's spirit have passed through the amulet? However they're arriving, though, the memories are unstoppable.

"What are you writing there?" Diana asks.

About the time I caught you and Karl having an affair.

"Nothing," Frankie says, closing her notebook.

Frankie can't even enjoy driving the golf cart. She's so distracted, she's afraid she's going to crash it.

During wool dyeing, Frankie thinks about how she can get Mr. Silvenus alone to talk to him. Then, a vision of her Latin teacher, again with the horns, the two of them walking through a market, the fishmongers wearing togas and sandals, her own sandals sticking to the bloody cobblestones.

She takes out her notebook. All day, the notebook. At lunch, she remembers the name of the orange cat she keeps thinking she sees on the steps. *Milo!* He purred so loudly. God, she loved that animal.

People eat and talk to her and Frankie nods along, pretending she's hearing what they're saying, fake laughing when it seems like something's supposed to be funny.

Levitating while distracted works less well. It's one thing when she's with Lonnie and he can lift the both of them, it's another when she's back with Eeva and neither of them can get their butts off the floor.

"Are you not feeling well, Frances?" Dr. Natas startles her, coming up from behind. "Maybe drink some water."

As she sips from the fountain, Frankie can't calm the shudder. Those feelings of doom she used to get around Dr. Natas, they're back, but different, because: *what he did to that sheep.* How can one person have the power to end life so effortlessly?

She's glad when Dr. Natas goes behind the veil. She remembers that, too. She can see the robes the Listeners wear, smell the fire being lit, hear the chanting.

"What do you think, Frank?"

It's her brother.

"Huh?"

"Will you stop writing in your book and be a *little* bit present?"

Panic, because she has no idea what's happening. The counselors, they're staring at her.

"What are you guys talking about?"

"The *spirits*," Lucie says. "That's all anyone's been talking about."

"Spirits? There can't be any spirits," Frankie says. "Those were bats."

"I went for a swim this morning and it was freezing cold," Efrat says. "I saw a shadow in the water."

"Nessie," Ox says. "I saw her, too."

"What?"

"Nessie—that's what they call the Loch Ness Monster."

They've already *named* the spirit? Now Frankie isn't remembering past lives, she's remembering last fall, catching all those shades. She can't deal with this right now.

"You need to teach us."

"Yeah, teach us!"

"Teach you *what*?" Frankie says.

"How to trap spirits."

"We're going to hunt this thing down tonight, mate," Ox says, and slams his horns into Lucie's.

"You can't hunt a spirit," Frankie says, suddenly angry. "You don't get to *choose* when you capture a spirit."

They look at each other, taken aback by how furious Frankie is.

"What is wrong with you?" Efrat says.

"You okay, sis?"

Omnia mutantur

"I'm not feeling well."

The spirits. The sisters always told her it was Dr. Natas releasing them; he said it was an earthquake. But what if they're here because of *her*? What if the spirits are connected to her getting these memories? She started getting the visions—the feelings of dread—as soon as she arrived, and that's when they started appearing, too. Wilma herself had said it, and Frankie just laughed it off.

It must be connected—it must ALL be connected!

Over dinner, Frankie can barely eat. Lonnie and Cadmus are

talking about the time they "borrowed" the Jaguar and it broke down in Chicago. The story sounds familiar. But does it really? Or is it the power of suggestion?

Under the table, Frankie flips through her notebook. God, her handwriting is bad. It looks like she scrawled this with her eyes closed.

She stops when she gets to *blue portable stereo.*

Portable record players—was that even a thing?

She asks Penny, maybe because Frankie thinks she's the least likely to remember.

"Oh yes!" Penny says. "With the turquoise case. We used to call it Ol' Blue Eyes."

"Because Mother loved to play Frank Sinatra on it, and we all hated him," Lonnie says.

"Who?" Frankie says.

"Ol' Blue Eyes!" Diana says. "You don't know Frank Sinatra? You even have his name!"

They all laugh. Why are they laughing?

22

Conversation with Silvenus

Mr. Silvenus always stays up late. Frankie's plan is to wait until everyone else goes to sleep to talk to him; that way there'll be no one to interrupt them or overhear. There's only one problem: *She* falls asleep. And dreams.

She's in the crypt. They're all there: Cadmus, Lonnie, Penny, Diana, Karl, Nasrat, and skinny Rodolfo Natas, looking like he did when he knocked on her door that first time. They put on the robes, like in her memory, and there's the same acrid smell of the fire being lit. The Listeners enter the inner chamber and gather in a circle around an altar. They begin a levitation, and the hum of their voices vibrates in her chest. Anxiety rises within her—she can't bear the vibrations—and in her dream she opens her eyes. Her gaze meets the empty stare of a skull on the altar. It's charred black, because of who it belonged to.

The Founder.

Frankie wakes. She has to run to the bathroom and is already vomiting as she whips up the toilet seat with a bang. Tears stream down her cheeks as she throws up more. The nausea is even more undeniable than when she ate the steak—that raw, bloody steak Sylvie's dad fed her, when she threw up for days. She flushes the toilet, then dry heaves. There's nothing more to throw up. The bathroom door opens. *I don't want anyone to see me like this.*

"How long have you been feeling sick?" Mr. Silvenus asks.

Instead of answering his question, Frankie thinks of the one she wants to ask. *Am I Mother?* But it sounds so ridiculous—especially to ask it here, kneeling in front of a toilet—that she can't bring herself to. So she asks a different one instead.

"Is it true about Pythagoras?" she says, coughing.

The teacher looks down at her.

"What about Pythagoras?"

"That he could remember his past lives."

His eyebrows push together, carving deep lines into his forehead.

"Why do you ask?"

You know why. She knows he knows. Frankie gets annoyed with him for playing games. That nightmare—of Mr. Silvenus grabbing her, shaking her, the world dying in a storm of ash. That *happened*. She's not sure where or when, but she knows that it did.

"Do you ever think about your horns?" Frankie asks, wiping her mouth with toilet paper, wiping her snot. She throws it in the bowl and flushes again.

Mr. Silvenus smiles feebly. He reaches into his hairline, right above his temples. "I can still feel them, sometimes."

"You were thinner then. Your hair was red, and curly." She stands up and puts down the seat. "I remember it, like, perfectly."

"Honestly, Frances, it might be better if you didn't."

"Believe me, I've been trying not to," she says.

"I want to spare you," Mr. Silvenus says. "I don't want to be the one to tell you."

"To tell me *what*?"

Mr. Silvenus sighs.

"That you're waking up."

―

Having an insane thought—an impossible theory—is one thing. Having it confirmed is something else entirely.

When she finally asks the question—"Am I Mother?"—it's like it is coming from the mouth of someone else, somewhere else. And when he responds, it's like she only hears the echo of what he's saying.

"You once were Mother. Her and many others."

"How many others?" Frankie wants to know. "How is this **possible**?"

Her heart races; she can't slow it.

Omnia mutantur

She's not listening to what Mr. Silvenus is saying.

So he waits.

Waits for her to come back to herself.

Waits for the bathroom to stop spinning.

Is it spinning for him, too?

༄

"This isn't the beginning, Frances."

Maybe it's the water Mr. Silvenus gave her that allowed her to calm down and finally hear him, or the big armchair in his apartment she's sitting in.

"You are waking up to a game you've been playing for two thousand years, in sixty-six different bodies."

"How do you know how many?"

"You keep track. You make diaries of your pasts," he says, pouring red wine for himself. The liquid goes glugging out of the bottle. "You're that kind of person."

Her moleskin journal—she thought it was such an original idea. That Mr. Silvenus knows something about her that she herself didn't realize is too bizarre.

"Why am I starting to remember?" Frankie asks. "Why now?"

Silvenus shakes his head like he's fighting himself.

"Thirteen, fourteen—this is the age when it begins. Sometimes earlier." Mr. Silvenus goes to put the cork back in the mouth of the bottle, then places it on the table. "Sometimes later."

Sixty-six lives. The number starts to sink in. "I've been through this sixty-six times?"

"Through remembering, sixty-five times," Mr. Silvenus says. "In the first life, you couldn't recall any of your past ones."

You know when someone says, *That's a lot to unpack.* This is a **lot** to unpack. So much, Frankie can't even begin. She wants to leave. To run. But she has more questions.

"Does it always start like this? With the nightmares? The visions?"

Mr. Silvenus takes a drink, nodding. "And the vomiting."

"The vomiting? That's a part of it?" she says. So it wasn't the bloody steak after all. "Is it like some kind of disease?"

"I wouldn't categorize past-life memory as an illness, Frances. Most call it a gift."

"*Sixty-six* lives," she says. "But I don't remember that many. Not nearly."

"They come back slowly, over time," Mr. Silvenus says. "You won't remember everything, of course. Certain lives you hardly remember at all."

"Most of what I remember is Mother."

"You always best remember your most recent life. And—so you've told me—your first one."

"The ash storm," she says. "The dream you're in."

"Not a dream. A memory."

"But how is that possible? It's like I'm in *The Hobbit* or something. And the world is ending."

"It seemed like it," Mr. Silvenus says. "And it was, I suppose, the end of *a* world."

"What world?"

"Pompeii," he says. "You're remembering the eruption of Mt. Vesuvius."

"Pompeii?" Frankie shakes her head. "Didn't that happen in, like, 200 BC or something?"

"Oh, not *that* long ago." Mr. Silvenus smiles. "It was only 79 AD."

"And you were there, in my dream—memory—whatever." He nods. "So are you like me? You get reincarnated?"

"No, that was this same old body," he says. "When the eruption started, I tried to get you to leave with me, but you wouldn't come. Not without your family."

"You're *two thousand years old*?"

"A bit older, actually," he says, tilting his head to one side. "My kind—we live long."

"So am I alone, or can anyone else remember their past lives?"

Mr. Silvenus stares at her. "What do *you* think?"

Think? That's the last thing Frankie wants to do. She's tired of thinking, of guessing—she wants to be told.

But she doesn't need to be. The answer is too obvious.

That dream—in the apartment, when she opens the door.

Rodolfo Natas. She knew he'd be coming. And Frankie knows what Mother was thinking: *This boy is the Founder.*

Frankie bursts into tears.

Mr. Silvenus holds her.

They've done this before.

"Hey, Mr. Silvenus, have you seen my sister?"

Lucie's voice is muffled through the door.

"I went to wake her up to start breakfast but she's not in her room."

"I haven't seen her," Mr. Silvenus says, staring at Frankie.

"Well, if you do . . . ," Lucie says. "Just tell her I'm looking for her, I guess."

Mr. Silvenus and Frankie listen to the footsteps get softer, the sound of the hallway door opening fast, closing slow. They can talk again, but what else is there to say?

Well, there's a lot else to say, but Mr. Silvenus wants to stop.

"You'll reject what I tell you," he says. "You'll reject *me*, and then you'll run away. This is what you always do."

Frankie hates him telling her what she's going to do, like she's performing some script that's already been written.

"You can't rush the process, Frances."

"Why do you call me that—Frances?" she says. "Why don't you call me Mother? Or Luna?"

Luna. She didn't remember until she said it.

That was her name—her *first* name.

In Pompeii.

I need to escape. Like I should have then. But instead of leaving with Silvenus, she went looking for her mother and sisters. God, it's like any other memory, but from two *thousand* years ago.

"I call you Frances because that's who you are," Mr. Silvenus says. "Mother—Luna—the others—they were different versions of you. Other lives. But they're not who you are in this one."

She stands up.

"I have to go."

Mr. Silvenus nods.

"Before you do," he says, and walks a few short steps to a painted landscape on the wall. The Latin teacher grabs it by the frame and lifts the hanging wire off the picture hooks. He places it face down on the table and tears the brown paper from the back, revealing a canvas stretcher. Taped to the wooden brace is an envelope. Mr. Silvenus peels it off and hands it to Frankie. Across the front is written:

To whom it may concern

"Who does it concern?" she asks.

"Who do you think, Frances?" Mr. Silvenus says, with a look like *Do I have to tell you everything?*

Frankie opens the envelope and unfolds the letter inside. The writing is in cursive, which—suddenly—she can read. She recognizes something else. The handwriting. It's hers. Meaning, Mother's.

Her heart thumps as she reads the letter, even though there's hardly anything to read. *Listen with your eyes, then with your mind, and only last with your ears.*

She's heard that saying before.

Uncle Sal.

Frankie has a sudden memory of him. Not from Great Adventure, or Thanksgivings with Mom, but here. In a classroom.

Uncle Sal taught at the Pythagorean Institute. He worked for Mother. She called him *Salvatore*.

What does it mean?

"Goodbye, Frances," Mr. Silvenus says.

At the door, she turns around.

"Were we friends?" she says. "In my past lives."

Mr. Silvenus smiles. "You're the only true friend I've ever had, Frances," he says. "Among the humans, anyway."

23
A Short Chapter

Approaching the front gate of the Institute, Frankie has the sudden premonition that she'll die if she walks through it. That she'll be like the sheep Dr. Natas put to sleep.

Is this the curse that keeps the sisters in the gym? That they can leave if they want to, but they'll die if they do?

Frankie's pretty sure that it is. And that Mother is the one who did it to them.

No wonder Not-Estelle hates me.

As she enters into the gap between the pillars of the thick stone walls, Frankie holds her breath, as if somehow this will keep her alive, as if what will kill her is the air. She feels like she did when she first put on the amulet, like she has lost control over her own body.

Out the other side, stepping foot onto the main road, Frankie exhales. She's not dead.

She takes out her cell phone and watches the screen as she walks, waiting to get in range of a signal.

Two bars flash on.

Frankie makes a call.

"I need your help."

INTERMEDIUS

Arriving at the door marked *Head of School*, the old satyr reaches to open it. An instant before his hand would have grasped the knob, however, it turns, as if the door were expecting him. *Channeling?*

No, Lucius.

"Mr. S." He nods, barely acknowledging his Latin teacher as he skirts around him. The boy's manner is so unusually abrupt that Silvenus wonders: *Could Frances have possibly told her brother?*

"Where is he off to in such a hurry?" the satyr asks, entering the office.

"Where is *she* off to is the question," Natas says grimly.

"Pardon?" Silvenus asks.

"The girl is gone. I felt it, and her brother confirmed it. He came to ask if I knew where she was." Natas looks the satyr up and down, like he's evaluating a horse at auction. "Did you know she left?"

"How would I know?" Silvenus says, playing innocent. "I don't possess whatever connection the two of you have."

Natas leans back in his chair. "We need to get her back."

"If she is gone and you try to force her back, she'll never return."

"I know that," Natas snaps.

Silvenus doesn't have a particular rationale for not telling Natas about his conversation with Frances, other than to avoid his wrath for not informing him immediately. Of course, the old satyr has been keeping the girl's confidences from the time she was

Luna and Latin wasn't the subject he was teaching her but Greek. (Latin, after all, was her first language.)

Were they friends! Such a question for her to have asked him. The things he wishes he could have told her—could have warned her of—but one cannot stop a child from making mistakes. What is vital is not repeating one's own past errors. Silvenus must have discipline. And faith in Frances, to make the correct choices.

Because nothing is predestined. Fate is an illusion, masking what are merely patterns. If he has learned one thing in all his years of watching the two of them, it is this.

For selfish reasons, the old satyr doesn't want a repeat of what happened in that one life of hers, oh so long ago, when he told her everything, and she left, and he had to wait seventy long years—until her next incarnation—to see her again. Silvenus never did find out what became of her that life, and she never spoke of it.

"If she is remembering, she might come back for Cadmus's sake," Silvenus says. "She was always fond of him."

"She had better hurry, then," Natas says. "The man might die at any moment."

An unkind thought, uttered unkindly. But Natas has been jealous of Cadmus across two lives. It is perhaps the most human part left of him.

"I never understood what she saw in him," Natas says.

"His ability, for one thing." Even when he was still a boy, Mother would go on about how Cadmus was the greatest channeler either of them had trained in generations. "She said he was more powerful than both sisters together."

Natas scoffs, pushing a *that's-an-understatement* breath through his nose. "And soon he will die and all that he ever learned will be erased, and he will be reborn the average child of a bus driver in Accra, or of a schoolteacher in Auckland. Or perhaps he will not be reborn human at all."

Schadenfreude, from the German word meaning malicious joy in the misfortune of others. Another human trait retained by Natas.

"Do any of these children have talent?" Silvenus asks. "The counselors."

"As a channeler? On *his* level?" Natas shakes his head.

"How about Efrat?" Silvenus says.

Again Natas shakes his head. "Her pride gets in the way of her potential."

"And the rest?"

"You know that is not why the others are here."

Indeed Silvenus does. "Except Wilma."

Now, Natas nods. "She is different, that one. She started so young," he says. "But the girl is difficult to read. Everyone else, they want to show off what they can do. Wilma hides."

Natas gets up suddenly, disgusted with himself for entertaining such idle talk. "Where can Frances be going?" he says, returning to the question he asked when the old satyr walked in.

Silvenus is puzzled by Natas. Surely he knows where the girl is going, or, at the very least, can make an excellent guess.

Patterns.

PART TWO

RETURNS

24

Road Trip

At the Wawa, Frankie almost breaks her vegetarianism to get a hot dog; the ones Sylvie and Mistral are getting look too good. Instead, she grabs a bag of dill pickle chips and a peach iced tea.

When the lady handing Mistral her hot dog says, "Is that all for you today?" Sylvie and Frankie bust out laughing. And again when they pay.

"What's wrong with you two?" Mistral says, pushing open the door with his back.

Outside, Sylvie shows Frankie how to pump gas, and they get in the truck. As Sylvie pulls out of the rest stop, Mistral puts on the middle seat belt and opens Google Maps.

"Wait! Turn here!"

"What?" Sylvie says.

"I mean—get to the left!" Mistral says.

"The road is dividing!" Frankie says. *Why would it do that?*

Sylvie misses the lane change, then un-misses it. Mountain Dew bottles roll across the floor.

"Do you see that truck!" Mistral shouts.

A tractor trailer honks, and Frankie worries she might get to her next life sooner than expected. The way Sylvie is driving, Frankie understands why sixteen-year-olds have driving restrictions.

More honking as the tractor trailer passes the truck and the driver curses at them through his rolled-down passenger-side window. Yet again, the girls burst into laughter.

"It's not funny!" Mistral says, which makes them laugh harder.

Thankfully, the next turn isn't for thirty miles. "Don't let him navigate anymore," Sylvie says.

Frankie switches the map app to the voice setting and puts on a playlist. Mistral leans over and turns up the stereo.

Frankie's first road trip with friends—this is *fun*.

"It's so crazy that we can just stop anywhere we want," Mistral says. "Like, we don't even have to ask an adult!"

Having a friend who's older is great. Unfortunately, Sylvie is only on her learner's permit, which means she's not supposed to drive without an adult in the car. But when Frankie called her this morning and said she had quit the retreat (she blamed Ox) and needed to get home, Sylvie volunteered. They met at Dink's house to ask if they could borrow his truck.

He didn't want to give it to them.

"Come on, how many times did *you* drive on a permit?" Sylvie said.

Dink gave in—grudgingly—and Mistral wanted to come along for the ride.

Out on the highway, Frankie has been able to put everything out of her mind for a few hours. A road trip is better than any mantra. If only Lucie wasn't constantly texting, asking where she is. She shut off her alerts a hundred miles ago, but still.

Welcome to New Jersey! Google says in an Irish accent as they cross the bridge over the Delaware River.

"Sixteen more *minnits*," Frankie says, copying the accent.

"Oh it's sixteen, *izzit*?" Sylvie says, doing the same thing.

"You guys are seriously bad at that," Mistral says.

Frankie can't wait to be home and sleep in her old bed, and she's hoping that being outside the walls will put a stop to the remembering. Most of all, though, Frankie just wants her mommy. The word sounds ridiculous—Mom has never been a mommy, but still. Things have been better lately.

Her one worry is that her mother will somehow find out what's going on. Frankie's embarrassed and doesn't want anyone to know about her past lives. Especially not Mom.

In five hundred feet, use the left-hand lane to turn left.

"Here?" Sylvie asks.

"Yeah," Frankie says.

Your destination is on the right.

Drops of rain dot the dirty windshield as Sylvie pulls to the curb.

"So is this where you grew up?" she asks.

Frankie nods, and the other two nod along with her.

"Nice," Mistral says.

"Not really," Frankie says. "But it's home."

The Prius is in the driveway, but unfortunately so is another car. Ron's.

"Do you think you'll come back to school in the fall?" Mistral asks.

"Either that or stay in Flemington and get a job at CVS," Frankie says. "Ten percent off makeup."

She's not even kidding.

"If you take the job, hook me up," Sylvie says.

"We better start driving back," Mistral says to Sylvie. "If your dad finds out we did this, you're grounded forever and I'm fired."

Grabbing her backpack, Frankie's heart sinks. She thanks Sylvie, gives her and Mistral a hug, shimmies out, and watches the taillights of Dink's truck streak away.

The smell of summer rain hitting pavement fills the air and, in an attempt to stay dry, Frankie stands under the tree in the front yard, the one with the roots lifting up the concrete sidewalk. While she tries to come up with a better story to explain leaving the retreat, Mom passes by the living room window and Frankie—

She's back in Mother's office. The one Dr. Natas has now, but it looks like it did when it belonged to her. Newspaper articles are pinned to a thumbtack board and the shelves are lined with encyclopedias.

Across the desk from her sits a young woman, fresh out of college, interviewing to be her administrative assistant—the school secretary. Frankie feels what Mother felt in the moment. *Is this girl smart enough? Will she work hard?* Frankie tries to see the young woman's face, but it's like trying to read a sign in your peripheral vision; you can see the letters, but you can't make out the words. The young woman's voice, though—Frankie would know that voice anywhere.

It's Mom's.

Frankie is remembering meeting her own mother.

25

Peripheral Visions

I met my *mom before I was born.*

As many times as she says it to herself, it still makes no sense. And Frankie didn't just meet her, she hired her. She was Mom's boss.

The memories flood back, and now she does clearly see her. Not at the job interview, but later, sticking her head through the door, telling her there's a phone call. "Thank you, Rose," Mother said.

Calling her mom by her first name—also weird.

What she can't get over is how much Mom looks like Lucie. Frankie didn't know she was ever that blond. Or young.

Not caring how wet she's getting, Frankie starts to walk and takes a turn onto a street where she doesn't know anybody—god forbid she runs into Stella, or worse, Serena. She chants her mantra as she goes, but what's the point? It's not working.

What does this mean? Why did Mom never say she worked at the Institute? Or that Uncle Sal worked there, too?

Frankie isn't sure she wants to know the answer.

At some point, she finds herself back in front of the house, the sound of whatever show Mom and Ron are watching spilling outside. Unable to bring herself to go in, Frankie takes out her phone.

Mom answers, surprised to hear from Frankie. "Is everything okay?"

How could you ever answer such a question?

"I just wanted to tell you I love you, Mom," Frankie says.

"Why, I love you, too, Frances," Mom says, even more surprised.

After Frankie hangs up, she dries her face. From the rain, except not only.

26
Patience and Fortitude

Frankie wakes up briefly in Philly, then sleeps hard all the way across Pennsylvania, getting up when the bus pulls into the station at Pittsburgh. With eighty minutes to make her transfer, she gets an iced coffee. Now it's lunch in Columbus, and she and her fellow passengers have to suffer a thirty-minute stopover on a black asphalt parking lot with no shade in Springfield, Ohio.

I thought this was supposed to be an express.

A phone call from Lucie. *Ignore.* Now, another flurry of texts.

LUCIE where are you?

LUCIE what is GOING ON?

LUCIE stop ghosting me!!

LUCIE everyone's really worried

> **LUCIE** should I call mom?

> **LUCIE** just text me k so I know you're not kidnapped

Frankie types

> **FRANKIE** k

and puts the phone away.

The first bus Frankie took went from the bagel shop in Flemington to New York Port Authority. With hours to kill before her midnight departure, Frankie walked to Times Square. When she came to see *Wicked*, Frankie thought it was the coolest place ever, but in her present mental state, the statue mimes and actors dressed as Disney characters freaked her out, so she kept going, eventually winding up at the New York Public Library. On either side of the grand staircase were stone lions that were way bigger than the griffins at school. The whole building was so incredibly grand, and so familiar. Did she come here as Mother? Or was it in some other past life?

No wait—she saw it in a Spider-Man movie.

Back at Port Authority, Frankie panicked trying to find the gate. Once she did, she stressed over whether the driver was going to ask for ID to prove she's sixteen, but she needn't have. The LA-bound Greyhound is pretty much the teen runaway express.

Not express.

On the bus, no one screams *All aboard*. Not in Manhattan, and not now in Ohio. You just have to know when to get on. The bus isn't all bad, though. There are chargers on the armrests, good Wi-Fi, and even better AC.

The reason that Frankie is going cross-country is to visit Uncle Sal. She doesn't have his number to text him (and isn't sure she would if she did), but she does have his address, from Mom making her write thank-you letters for the one-hundred-dollar check he sends every Christmas.

Back in her seat, Frankie goes into her map history and clicks on street view. Sal's house looks seriously nice. She's psyched at the thought of staying there. Assuming he'll let her, of course.

Not that this is a vacation; Frankie wants to see her uncle because of the letter Mother left. *Listen with your mind.* Maybe Sal can explain what it means. And other stuff, too. Like, did her grandparents *really* die in a car accident? Why did Mom have no pictures of them? The idea that all her old photos were ruined in a flood is a little too convenient. Couldn't she get copies?

If he's even at this house, Frankie thinks as she zooms in on the car in the front yard, because what if Uncle Sal isn't real? Not her real uncle, she means. Do high school history teachers drive Teslas? What if those checks were sent by someone else? Frankie doesn't trust anything right now.

On the other hand, what if she gets to California and Uncle Sal *is* her uncle, and everything Mom said is true? That's the nicest thought of all.

⁕

Swordfish heads on the ends of spears tower above the market crowd, the peak of Vesuvius behind them. Every stall has one, the fishmongers competing for whose has the longest bill. They yell at her in Latin; not Ovid's Latin, but some other kind she understands better.

Fresh from the sea, my lady! I wrestled the beast myself!

Turning to face the bay, a calm breeze flutters her robe. She loves this view of the port, but something is off. Where are the boats? Turning back toward the fishmongers, the swordfish heads are gone and the market is abandoned. Ash hangs in the air. And what happened to the mountain? The top is gone.

Frankie gasps, waking up.

She's on a bus. *Right*. She gets self-conscious, wondering who heard her. Like anyone would care. Some guy is sleeping in the aisle. To make it to the bathroom, she had to climb over two seats to get past him.

Pulling her journal out of her backpack, Frankie writes about the swordfish heads. She's logged a bunch of new memory fragments—some stuff about meeting Mom, but more and more of her entries come from her life as Luna.

Curious (and with nothing else to do), Frankie image searches *what did pompeii look like*. She scrolls through cheesy reconstructions of the city, then clicks on the related *pompeii bodies*, bringing up dozens of photos of people caught dying in the eruption.

*These can't be the **actual** bodies*, Frankie thinks, except they kind of are. Archaeologists made plaster casts in the voids left by people when the ash that buried them hardened into rock and their flesh turned to dust. Because their skeletons didn't disintegrate, bits of bone and teeth gruesomely protrude from the plaster, each person a mummy statue frozen in the exact, agonizing moment of their death.

There are men splayed out, holding up arms to protect themselves from the falling rocks; a woman crouched as she gets smothered; a horse fallen to its side; a dog on its back; and a group of three people huddling, holding each other. They're the most gorgeous, grotesque, moving images that Frankie has ever seen.

Did she know any of these people? What if her body—if Luna's body—is one of them? Then it hits Frankie. There are *sixty-five* dead bodies of hers, somewhere. And the bones of at least one of them is in the crypt.

Frankie closes her browser, moves the seat back, and puts on her *Get Happy Eighties Music* playlist.

Is Missouri really a state? The name sounds made up. Frankie had to memorize the capitals of all fifty states in fourth grade and she's pretty sure Missouri wasn't one of them.

At the rest stop, she gets french fries—again. French fries and potato chips, stop after stop, because what else is she going to eat? Vegetarianism and riding the Greyhound do not go hand in hand. (Not that she could afford a burger, anyway. She's already spent both her summer paychecks.)

Another call from Lucie. Then the texts.

LUCIE where are you?

LUCIE everyone's asking

LUCIE answer sis!

FRANKIE i'm on a greyhound bus

She's not even sure why she finally tells him, other than she's bored.

LUCIE what? a bus? seriously??

FRANKIE the wifi is rlly good

LUCIE are you some kind of teen runaway now?

LUCIE the police will come looking for you!

FRANKIE no one is sending the police

FRANKIE believe me

LUCIE when are you coming back?

LUCIE everyone misses you

LUCIE and you're missing carding

FRANKIE i don't even like playing spit

LUCIE carding is combing out wool

FRANKIE i was kidding

Lucie really doesn't get her sense of humor.

❧

How can there be *another* night on the bus? And how can someone be snoring *this loudly*? There's no way she'll sleep. Especially not in this seat. No matter what she does, she can't get comfortable. A bone in her butt has gone numb that she didn't even know she had. Maybe that guy lying in the aisle knew what he was doing.

Yawning, Frankie opens Pinterest, but she's barely updated her boards since going off to boarding school. They belong to yet another past life—emo seventh-grade Frankie.

Switching apps, she pulls up her book. If there's anything that'll put her to sleep, it's this.

By "her book," Frankie means the one she wrote. That Mother wrote.

Frankie discovered *Nature, Nurture, Narrative* when she was googling Mother's real name, *Zheng Mei*. She knew Mother was a psychologist, but not that she had written an actual book. Frankie likes that she did cool things in her past life.

In the introduction, Mother writes about how biology (*Nature*) and environment (*Nurture*) can't account for all of what forms a human being.

> <u>Narrative</u>—the stories we tell ourselves of who we are—is a third, less explored factor that shapes the personalities of human beings.

By page three, Frankie starts to fall asleep, because this is the densest, driest text she's ever tried to read. Could she possibly have been this boring?

Sorry, former me.

It still is cool she wrote a book, though.

27
Uncle Sal

Caridi/Lopez.

Frankie has been sitting on the curb for an hour, staring. It's so strange to see her own last name on this random mailbox, next to some random other last name, in front of this random house. The side of the mailbox has little birds painted on it and stands on the edge of the loveliest flower garden she's ever seen, which fits in perfectly with Pasadena, the loveliest place she's ever been.

"Frances? Is that *you*, Frances?"

Frankie wondered if she'd even recognize Uncle Sal, but of course she does. She gets up off the curb to hug him.

He's surprised and delighted. "Frances! I can't believe it!" Uncle Sal says. "The last time I saw you . . ."

"It was Great Adventure."

"Was it?" he says. "No—it was cousin Mike's wedding. In Bucks County."

Oh right. She forgot about that. God, she can't even remember *this* life, how is she ever going to remember the other sixty-five?

Frankie has been rehearsing all the questions she wants to ask her uncle, but she can't get a word in edgewise.

"How's your mother? And your brother?" Sal says, punching in the code for his alarm system. "You look so much older! And taller! Let me cook you dinner. What do you like?"

"Anything that wasn't an animal," Frankie says. "Or a potato."

"Risotto!" Rooting around his big, fancy refrigerator, he asks, "So, how do you and Lucie like the Institute?"

Frankie is surprised. "You knew we're going there?"

"Of course," he says, taking out a leek and some celery. "Your mom told me when you guys got in."

"So did you, like, know about the Institute before?" Frankie says, fishing.

"Well, I *did* work at the place for ten years," he says, taking out a cutting board and knife. "I helped your mom get her job there."

That made so much sense.

"So, you're my *real* uncle?" she says. "Not my, quote-unquote, 'uncle'?"

"Well yeah! What do you mean?" Sal looks up from what he's chopping. "Is this because I haven't been back to visit? I'm so sorry, I'm a *terrible* uncle. Seven years! I—"

"No, no," Frankie says. "It's just that Mom doesn't talk about our family. I've never even seen a photo of my grandparents."

A look like he understands comes to Uncle Sal's face and he wipes his hands on his apron, leaving the kitchen. He comes back with a laptop, open to Photos.

"Are these them?" Frankie says.

"From right after they were married."

"Wow, Lucie and Mom look *so much* like our grandmother." Frankie looks more like their grandfather, with the dark hair and dark eyes. "Why didn't Mom get copies of these photos from you after the flood?"

"After our folks died in the accident, your mom, well . . ." Sal keeps chopping. "I don't think she could bear to think about them."

So the car crash was real, too.

As Frankie scrolls through photos, Sal sautés the vegetables. They sizzle.

"Frankie," he says, "why are you here?"

The frying leeks and celery smell good.

"This is gonna sound crazy, but . . ." She pauses. "That time at Great Adventure, you told me this saying. And I found out Mother said it, too. You know Mother, right?"

"Yeah, I know Mother." Uncle Sal gives a fake half laugh. "And I know all about her sayings. *One person can change lives— but a school can change the world.*"

"It wasn't that one," Frankie says. "It was *Listen with your eyes, then with your mind,*"—Uncle Sal joins her—"*and only last with your ears.*"

He gives another half laugh. "Yeah, that was her favorite," he says, banging the wooden spoon against the side of the cast iron pan.

⁓

By the time Uncle Sal finishes making dinner, a couple things have become clear.

One, he has zero inkling that Frankie is the reincarnation of his former employer.

And two, he was never in the cult.

"I mean, sure, I knew about all that flying yogi stuff—I read the article online—but Ramakrishna died years before I got there," Sal says as they sit down to eat. "They still held their summer thing, but I was never around for that. We weren't allowed to stay on campus once school ended."

"And Mom?" Frankie asks. "Was she in the cult?"

Frankie wants the answer to be *no*.

Sal blows on his forkful of risotto. It's really, really hot.

"You should probably talk to her about that."

"She's not always honest about stuff," Frankie says. *Like never.* "She didn't even tell me she worked at the school."

Uncle Sal finally takes a bite, and chews. Slowly.

"Your mother was searching for something. Spiritually, I mean," he says. "So when Rudy asked her if she wanted to attend the summer retreat, she—"

"Rudy? Who's Rudy?"

"Natas. Rodolfo," Uncle Sal says with a sly smile. "He hated being called Rudy."

Frankie files that nugget of information away.

"So you knew Dr. Natas?"

"Well, sure. Mother adopted him while I was there. Don't ask me why she did or where he even came from, but . . ." Uncle Sal is flustered. "Look, I didn't ask questions. It wasn't my place. And I barely knew Rudy. The kid went off to Harvard when he was *fifteen*." Sal shakes his head.

Frankie can't imagine Dr. Natas being her age. "What was he like?"

"Brilliant, obviously. A little strange. I mean, I've been

working with teenagers a long time, but I never met anyone like him. He put us teachers to shame. Not just because he was smarter, but because he knew what you were thinking." Sal points his fork at his head. "What you'd say before you spoke."

That's for sure.

"Didn't you still think it was strange when a teenager started running the cult?" Frankie says. "And that your sister joined it?"

Uncle Sal looks down at the food he's moving around his plate. "I didn't think it *was* a cult, just a wellness retreat or something. When I came back to the Institute that fall, Rose was all Natas this and Natas that. And I kept saying to her, he's just some kid, and she said, no, he's the *one*."

"The *one*?" Frankie says.

"Like the Dalai Lama or something. I said, *You mean he's the next reincarnation of the Buddha?* And that was the end. She wouldn't talk anymore about it, because I wasn't taking it seriously. Everything became a big secret." He shakes his head. "Mother had just died, or everything would've been different. She wouldn't have allowed your mom to be at that retreat. She always kept the school separate from the yogi stuff."

Mother wouldn't have let Mom be in the cult? There's irony in there somewhere.

"I was upset with Rose for getting involved," Sal says, "and I felt guilty about her coming to the Institute in the first place. And then when she adopted you, well—"

"Adopted me?"

Adopted?

Adopted!

Sal's face is frozen in shock, his mouth open. Does her face look like that, too?

"You didn't know." His fork clinks against the plate. "Frances, I am so sorry for you finding out like this."

"Frankie," she says. "People call me *Frankie*."

"I had no idea it was a secret," he says. "If I'd been around you guys more, I would've known."

"Don't apologize. It's *her* fault for lying to me."

"Please don't blame your mother."

"Don't *blame* her?" Frankie says. "She lies about everything! She told us she had never even *met* Dr. Natas! That she had never been to the school!"

"Well, maybe she wanted to forget that part of her life."

"Forget?" Frankie says. "Then why send us there?"

"Because of Lucie, because where else—"

"She told me she gave birth to me! She told me the IVF story a thousand times!" Frankie wants to scream. Maybe she *is* screaming.

Is my whole life a lie? Is nothing Mom and Dr. Natas said to her true? Not that Dr. Natas even matters. It's *Mom's* job to take care of her!

Once she calms down—at least a little—Frankie asks Sal details about her adoption, but he doesn't know any. He had quit working at the Institute by then.

"Mom *never* told you where I came from?"

"She told me different things, to be honest," Sal says. "I wasn't able to get a straight answer."

"Sounds like Mom."

For a moment, there's an uncomfortable silence. Then Sal says, "Jamie and I want to adopt."

"Who's Jamie?"

"He's my partner," Sal says. "He's traveling for work."

"Well, make sure to tell your kids you didn't give birth to them," Frankie says, and starts eating the risotto.

28

Embracing Motherhood

This is the most comfortable bed ever and the sheets must have a thread count of ten million. After four nights on a bus, she should be sleeping like it's heaven, but she can't sleep at all.

Not because of the nightmares. She wants to dream of another life, is *trying* to remember being Mother, Luna, a hawk—anyone other than the daughter of Rose Caridi.

Frankie is mad at herself for having called Mom to tell her she loved her. What a joke! Like her mother *ever* loved her! She only loved Lucie. And now Ron. Goofy, white-haired, so-not-tall Ron!

At least Frankie finally knows why Mom always treated her like an orphan stepchild—because that's what she is!

It's the lying that bothers her most, after Mom promised she was done lying. Did she know all along that Frankie was Mother? *Of course she knew.* Mom knew about everything.

I don't care if I never talk to Mom again, Frankie tells herself as she rolls to the other side of the bed. She's not even Frankie anymore, or not only. She's Mother. And Luna. And everyone else she ever was. She's part of something way bigger than this family.

If only she could remember herselves better.

29
I Know Who You Really Are

Universal Studios. The Hollywood Walk of Fame. The Santa Monica Pier. The La Brea Tar Pits. Frankie *has* gone on vacation after all. Her LA tour guide isn't her uncle, however, but his partner Jamie.

Frankie loves Jamie. He works some fancy tech job, dresses like a Uniqlo model, and is the most California person she's ever met. He's enthusiastic about everything, most especially food.

"You've *got* to try Ethiopian if you're a vegetarian. Have you ever eaten it?"

She says no, but at the restaurant, she realizes she has, whether as Mother or in some other life she doesn't know. It's foggy.

The memories most clearly coming back are of Sal. He tells a joke, and Frankie remembers the punch line. He holds a cup of coffee, and she knows he's going to squint as he takes a sip. When he nods to her, she's back in the halls of the Institute walking to her office. Sal is both her uncle and a former work colleague; the weirdest thing is how not weird it is.

She texts Lucie.

> **LUCIE** You're with Uncle Sal?! No way!

> **FRANKIE** Did you know he has a boyfriend?

> **LUCIE** Uncle Jamie! I'm soooo jealous you're getting to meet him!!

It burns Frankie that Mom told Lucie about Jamie and not her. She wants to forget about their mother all over again. If only Sal would let her.

"What should I tell your mom when I talk to her?"

"Why do you have to tell her anything?"

"I feel bad lying about you being here."

"How is it lying?" Frankie says. "It's not like she's gonna ask. She has no idea I'm here, and Lucie promised not to tell her."

"You guys are allowed to have your *own* relationship, you know," Jamie says, then changes the subject. "Tell me more stories about this Mother person. I can't believe I've never heard them."

Frankie has been asking Uncle Sal about her, at first to jar her memory, now because she likes to hear about how smart she was.

"Mother was the kind of person who knows more about your specialty than you do," he says. "My master's thesis was on Venetian naval power in the fifteenth century, and when I went to Dubrovnik—"

"Ragusa," Frankie says, not meaning to correct him, but doing so all the same.

Dumbstruck, Sal stares at her.

"That's *exactly* what Mother would say. She corrected me

every time." He grabs the table to steady himself, then leans across it. "Why would *you* say that?"

"I—I don't know," Frankie says, scrambling. "We've been studying it at school, I guess?"

"You've been studying how *Dubrovnik* used to be called *Ragusa*?"

Frankie can't think of what to say.

Sal gives her a hard stare. The moment is tense to the point of excruciating. "Mother was the only person who would say that."

"Well, clearly not the *only*," Jamie says, laughing and grabbing Sal's shoulder. "I think all this going down memory lane is a little much for you, babe."

Frankie is sure Sal has figured out who she is. Then, "That school!" he says. "I'm so glad I got out of there. Weird stuff like this happened all the time. I swear there were *ghosts* there."

"Ghosts!" Jamie laughs again.

If only you knew, Frankie thinks.

◦∽◦

They just left a cool vintage shop in Silver Lake and Frankie can't wait to wear what she got. The cutoffs look like the kind Penny and the other hippie girls wore at the Institute, way back when. Mother hated their style, but not Frankie.

Having arrived with one extra outfit stuffed in her backpack that she changed in and out of at bus stop bathrooms, Frankie needed new clothes. Jamie insisted on buying them for her, including a vintage rock shirt that cost $125. He was an even better shopper than tour guide, and helped Frankie work out a look that suited the new her better. Not the one who remembers her past lives, but the one who doesn't hide inside XL black hoodies.

"They have the best carne asada tacos," Sal says.

More food. This time from a truck. The cutoffs will have to wait.

"Frankie's a *vegetarian*, babe." Jamie turns to her. "Don't worry. The jackfruit birria tacos here are uh-mazing! There's a reason there's always a line."

And not just a line, but a line with celebrities on it. Because Frankie recognizes an actor from a show she and Lucie used to watch. She's so excited she has to text him right away. And for once, her brother texts right back.

> **LUCIE** I know who you really are

Frankie's heart drops. She gets out of the taco truck line to call him.

"What do you mean?" she asks as soon as he answers the phone, wanting to make sure they're talking about the same thing. "*Who* do you think I am?"

"Don't make me say it, Frank," Lucie says. "It's too freaking bizarre."

Isn't that the truth?

What can Frankie say to him? Where should she even begin? She looks back at her uncles, moving up the line.

"Look, I have to call you later," Frankie says, "but was it Mr. Silvenus who told you about me? Or Dr. Natas?"

"Neither," Lucie says. "It was Wilma."

"*Wilma?*"

"Yeah," he says. "She's, like, really worried about you. She wants you to come back."

"But how does Wilma know?"

"I'm, uh, pretty sure all the Listeners know," Lucie says. "I kinda think you're why they're here."

"Do you want it spicy?"

Frankie practically jumps out of her skin.

"Did I scare you?" Uncle Sal says. "Sorry!"

Frankie tells him yes spicy, and as soon as he's back out of earshot she says to her brother, "How are *you* taking it? Are you upset?"

"Why would *I* be upset?" Lucie says. "I'm just worried about you, sis."

Frankie can think of a million reasons why Lucie would be upset. Why can't he ever think about himself? It's actually annoying.

Lucie promises to keep her past-life identity a secret from the other counselors—"None of them would believe it, anyway"—and asks Frankie when she's coming back.

"We're done carding the wool," he says. "Tomorrow we start spinning it into thread."

"Well, I can't miss that," Frankie says.

As she walks over to the bench where Uncle Sal and Jamie are eating their tacos, Frankie opens the Greyhound schedule on her phone.

30
Frankie Reads Herself

"**I'm not going** to have the niece I just met take another *bus* across the country," Jamie said as he tapped the buy button on a first-class Amtrak ticket.

No one sleeps in the aisles and the scenery is way better than on the Greyhound, but the train Wi-Fi sucks. Not that Frankie cares, because she's got something better than her phone: a book.

Nature, Nurture, Narrative

"Are you sure I can have it?" she said.

"Oh yeah, Mother gave me a whole box of them," Uncle Sal said, surprising her with a copy at the train station. "I don't think she sold many . . ."

If the book seemed boring when she tried to read it on her phone, she's totally into the hardcover. Because of what it explains.

Frankie underlines:

No one "authentic self" exists, no singular person within each of us waiting to be discovered.

Of course, she's underlining practically the whole book.

We create our self through narrative, the subjective story of our lives a quilt we stitch together using scraps of selected memory.

The words send a chill up Frankie's spine. Not just because they're true—we are our memories!—but because she knows the line that's coming before she even reads it. She remembers the words entering her brain, the sound of the typewriter keys clacking, the smell of the whiteout when she made a mistake, the taste of the coffee she drank when she unspooled a page to read it over.

Coffee. Of course she liked coffee. Tea—that was what the Founder drank, what Natas drinks, not her.

Frankie is reading the book to know who Mother was. She doesn't need a letter to herself; she wrote a whole *book* to herself. And it tells her that the secret to who you are isn't your genes or the family you were born into.

You are the story you make of yourself, Frankie writes on the top of the page. In cursive.

31
Table for Three

Pulling into the stop, Frankie gets up and grabs her bag. She had to switch from the train to a bus in Pittsburgh, but she's over an hour away from school and is going to have to spend the Christmas money Sal advanced her on an Uber since Sylvie can't pick her up. (When her dad found out she borrowed Dink's truck, he took away her driver's permit.) Stepping off the bus, though, Frankie sees she already has a ride.

Dr. Natas and Mr. Silvenus are waiting for her.

When Mr. Silvenus starts waving, Frankie bursts into laughter.

"Why are you laughing?" he says, hugging her.

"The two of you—at a bus stop? I mean, seriously," Frankie says. "And the way you're dressed. That *hat* . . ." She looks at her Latin teacher's cap, then to what Dr. Natas is wearing. "And I don't know about that jacket, Rudy."

"Ex*cuse* me?"

Mr. Silvenus grins.

"Never call me that again," Dr. Natas growls, turning around to walk to the Jaguar.

༺༻

"'Tis grand!" Mr. Silvenus shouts, leaning forward from the tiny back seat of the convertible. "Together again at last!"

Having the top down is super cool, but the wind—Frankie has to pull the hair out of the corner of her mouth to talk.

"How did you guys know I was going to be there?"

"You and I have the ability to find each other, even outside the walls," Dr. Natas says loudly.

"Plus Lucius told us which bus you'd be on!" Mr. Silvenus hollers.

Dr. Natas grits his teeth.

"We were surprised when he told us you were coming back!" Mr. Silvenus goes on. "Normally when you run off, it's for months! Even years!"

"Sometimes you never come back," Dr. Natas says.

Frankie should be angry with Dr. Natas, but she can't be. They've been doing this for two thousand years, so there must be a method to the madness, however messed up all his gaslighting has been. Besides, Frankie needs answers from him. "About my past lives."

"About *what*?"

"Past lives!" she says louder.

Dr. Natas shakes his head. "First, food," he says.

The only place with decent reviews is a restaurant called O'Malley's. Seeing these two sitting in a green leather booth is at least as strange as seeing them at the bus stop, but there *is* something grand about being with them. A good kind of déjà vu.

"This reminds me of when we used to go to that tavern in Pompeii," Mr. Silvenus says. "With the soups."

Frankie remembers it—the long marble counter, the bright animal murals on the walls. She can even taste the food.

"It's not like that at all," she says. "This place smells like onion rings and beer. There the food smelled amazing."

"You remember it?" Dr. Natas says.

"Nicias," Frankie says, the name coming to her. "He used to serve us."

"Indeed," Dr. Natas says. "He was the owner."

To be able to talk about the memories popping up—and get confirmation they're real—is thrilling to Frankie.

"Do you know what happened to him?" she asks. "Like, can you tell what other people get reincarnated into?"

"Of course not," Dr. Natas says. "How could I know such a thing?"

"Pythagoras did," Frankie says, shrugging.

Dr. Natas gives her a hard look. "Just how much of your pasts do you remember?"

With a smile she can't suppress, Frankie takes her moleskin diary out of her backpack and slides it across the table, and then a marble notebook. "I had to buy this in LA because I filled up the journal," she says, impressed with herself.

He's not.

"This is *it*?" Dr. Natas says, flipping through pages. "This is all you remember?"

"There's a lot in the second one," Frankie says, tapping the notebook.

"It's all the same two lives," he says. "How about Persia? How about Brazil? The War of the Spanish Succession?"

She starts to feel bad.

"Helene Margot?" he says.

"Who?"

Dr. Natas clicks his tongue in disgust.

"Stop overwhelming the girl," Mr. Silvenus says. "What do you expect?" He turns to Frankie. "Don't fret. This is always the way. He remembers his lives perfectly, from a very young age. You remember yours slowly, from an older age. And never completely. This frustrates him, because despite having grown to adulthood hundreds of times, he remains in every life an impatient *child*."

"Wait—hundreds?" Frankie says. "How far back can he remember?"

"He claims to have helped build the pyramids," Mr. Silvenus says. "So more than twice as long as you."

"Can we order?" Dr. Natas holds up his menu and taps on it, trying to get the waitress's attention.

"Do you see?" Mr. Silvenus says. "Impatient child."

"I need to eat," Dr. Natas says. "And to get them to turn down this air-conditioning. I swear it is the most despicable human invention since the steam engine."

"I disagree with you on that," Mr. Silvenus says.

"You two bicker like an old married couple," Frankie says.

"Spend two thousand years with someone, and you get on each other's nerves," Dr. Natas says.

"I tell you, it's a relief when he dies and I get a few years of peace," Mr. Silvenus says. "Sadly, he always finds me."

As they order, Frankie wonders if Dr. Natas is just hangry. What happened to the patient, kind, mentoring head of school? Or is that all an act?

Of course it is.

When the waitress leaves, Frankie leans across the table. "Now," she whispers, "tell me about my *past lives*."

"Tell you?" Dr. Natas arches an eyebrow. "What makes us unique, Frances, is that we have the power to re*call* our lives. We don't need others to explain them to us."

"Don't listen to him," Mr. Silvenus says, clearing the water glasses between him and Frankie. "That it takes time for you to remember isn't a flaw—it's what makes you human." He looks at Dr. Natas with disgust. "More human than him, anyway."

"What do *you* know about past lives? You remember only your present one, and sometimes not even that," Dr. Natas says. "The last time I found her, she was younger than she is now, and she knew who I was the moment we met. I thought per*haps* the process of remembering had sped up." He makes a sour face. "Obviously not."

"Do you mean the moment that you—the Founder—came to

Shanghai, right after the Japanese invasion," Frankie says, "to bring me to the Institute?"

"See?" Mr. Silvenus says. "She remembers."

Actually, she doesn't; she read it in the bio of Mother's book.

Dr. Natas gets increasingly annoyed by Frankie's questions, giving her nothing. Mr. Silvenus tries to be helpful, but her past-life names might as well have been randomly generated for all Frankie connects with them, let alone the events he's talking about.

He keeps going on about the time she was born in Martinique and changed her name to Helene Margot to fight in the War of the Spanish Succession. It feels like she missed a week of classes and is trying to catch up for a history test that she's totally going to fail.

"Why would I change my name to Helene Margot to be a soldier?"

"Excellent question! This is where—"

"Will you both stop? We cannot explain two thousand years of existence over a grilled cheese and tomato soup," Natas says, pushing his bowl away. "Enough with the questions, and enough with these sim*plistic* summaries. We need to get the check and get back to the Institute."

"Fine. Just tell me *one* thing, and be honest," Frankie says. "In my former lives, was I ever a princess?"

Mr. Silvenus shakes his head like *here we go*.

"Everyone thinks they must have been born into royalty in their former lives, or at the very least ex*tremely* wealthy. Let me tell you how it *really* was." Dr. Natas wags a butter knife at Frankie. "You were the maid. You were the peasant. You were the washerwoman. Your father beat you; your mother beat you. You were born poor and desperate in every single one of your lives because, until about a hundred years ago, ninety-nine percent of the world was poor and desperate. Even today, feasting on this disgusting cornu*copia* of calories at this r*idiculously* non-Irish Irish pub places you in the most fortunate tier of humanity, which is the saddest statement of all."

"I actually think their veggie burger is quite good," Mr. Silvenus says, taking another bite.

"There is a reason for the saying *Life is nasty, brutish, and short*."

"I never heard that saying," Frankie says.

"Yes, you *have*." Dr. Natas stabs the table with the butter knife. "You have repeated it to me in at least three lives."

"Ground rules," Frankie says. "Don't do that."

"Do what?" Dr. Natas says, leaning back and letting the knife fall to the table.

"Blame me for things in other lives I don't remember."

Dr. Natas raises an eyebrow again. "As you hardly remember anything, this might not be possible."

"I remember that I don't like that tone of voice or this eyebrow raise thing you do." Frankie throws her green napkin on the table as she gets up. "I've got to go to the bathroom."

When she comes back, Dr. Natas is tapping at his iPhone in confusion, with Mr. Silvenus kibitzing. They're trying to pay the bill.

Frankie tells them what to do and, when they still can't figure it out, pulls the phone away in frustration.

"Tap *here* when the link comes up," she says. "You know the secrets of eternity but you can't work a QR code? God, you're old."

"I am *not* old," Dr. Natas says. "I'm thirty-three."

"First, that *is* old, and second, you're like five thousand."

Dr. Natas grits his teeth and gets up from the table.

"Let us go," he says. "There are people who have been waiting sixteen years for what is about to occur."

"Which is?" Frankie asks.

"The return of Mother," Dr. Natas says, pushing the door open.

Hot air bursts into the restaurant while Frankie looks back at Mr. Silvenus for explanation.

"The Listeners await," he says with a smile.

32

Transition

As far as she's concerned, the Listeners can keep awaiting—all she wants to do is collapse onto her bed. But that has to wait, too, because when Frankie walks into the dorm, the other kids are waiting for her in the common area. They crowd around and hug her, and Frankie can't resist a huge smile.

"Why is everyone here?" she says, asking the most stupidly obvious question.

"To welcome you back!" Moira says.

"We were worried about you, sis," Lucie says.

Wilma flashes a smile, hanging back behind everyone else.

Now, questions from all directions: "Why did you leave?"

"Where did you go?" "Are you back for good?" "Were you actually in Los Angeles?" "Did you for real see celebrities?"

Ek steps in to save her, making like Argus herding sheep.

"Come on, you guys," he says, leading the students toward their rooms. "Frankie needs to get some sleep. We'll see her in the morning."

"Will we, mate?" Ox says. "They're gonna fire her, yeah?"

"That's not the Pythagorean Institute way . . . ," Ek says, their voices fading down the hallway.

Only Lucie and her old roommate remain, and now Wilma hugs Frankie. Wilma's not only never hugged her, Wilma has never said hello or goodbye before. Frankie gets it; she doesn't like transitions, either. Still, it feels awkward to have Wilma gripping her so tightly.

"Don't leave me like that again," Wilma says, finally letting go. As she pushes the front door to leave, she turns to give Frankie an ironic fang smile, but it's half-hearted.

Frankie and her brother watch Wilma head up toward the Mothership, in and out of the darkness between the lights that line the brick walkway.

"When she told me who you were, I didn't believe it," Lucie says, shaking his head. "I went and stared at that painting of Mother for two hours. It was so weird to think, *That's you.*" He turns to look at Frankie. *"That's my sister."*

"It's weirder for me."

"The thing is, I can totally see it," Lucie says. "In your eyes. And definitely the smile, like how you don't really smile for a picture."

It's true; Frankie can't fake smile. She's not sure if it's out of a refusal to please people or if she's physically incapable.

"The expression," Lucie says. "That portrait has *your* expression."

Her brother is going someplace with this, but Frankie can't figure where.

"What are you trying to say, Lucie?"

He shrugs. "Just, how am I supposed to act around you?" he says. "You're *her*. And like . . . other people, too?"

"And animals. Don't forget the animals," Frankie says. "I've been a squirrel five times."

Lucie's eyes go wide. "Really?"

"Nah," she says. "I mean, maybe. Honestly, I don't remember all that much. Dr. Natas is mad at me for how much I don't."

"Dr. Natas, mad?" Lucie says, surprised. "But he's, like, *Mister* Patient."

"Yeah, well . . . ," Frankie says, and doesn't finish the sentence. "Look, Luce, it's not Freaky Friday in here. Some other person didn't wake up in my body. I'm still me. I'm still your big sister."

Lucie brightens up. "So you'll still make fun of me?"

"I'll *never* stop doing that," Frankie says. "I promise."

33

Anticipation

6:07 a.m.

The summer retreat should feel different, because Frankie's very understanding of her own existence is different. Yet here she is at Chapel, washing the coffee filter, scooping out the grounds, and pouring water into the machine. Things are the same as before she went across the country, before she read Mother's book, before she confronted Mr. Silvenus and Dr. Natas.

"Slice the bread for the toaster," Efrat says. "And microwave the butter from the freezer."

Just the same.

7:39 a.m.

Frankie can feel their eyes. They flit over the rim of orange juice glasses to sneak a look at her, and up from spoons scooping muesli.

The Listeners know what's coming this afternoon—that Frankie is going behind the veil for her ceremony. That *Mother* is.

The only one acting relaxed is Cadmus. "Would you pass me the maple syrup, Frances?" he says with an amused smile.

As much as Frankie is looking forward to her big reveal, she's feeling anxious, too. Mostly, she just wants it to happen already. Why does the day have to be going so *slow*?

8:21 a.m.

"*Beep beep!*" Ek says as he zips by on the golf cart. The old hippies wave, Penny sitting shotgun and Diana and Lonnie on the back.

As the counselors return the wave, Moira leans into Frankie's ear. "We found out that Lonnie used to be married to *Penny*. They have two kids together," she whispers. "She left him for some Italian movie director and then he married her best friend, Diana."

Right! Frankie remembers that. Mother totally disapproved.

"But now the three of them live in one house," Lucie says. "Penny moved in with them once she couldn't take care of herself."

"I told you they were a throuple," Ox says.

"Taking care of your ex-wife and your best friend when she gets dementia doesn't mean you're in a throuple," Lucie says.

"I don't know what else you'd call it, mate."

Frankie asks if they found out anything more about the Mysterions.

"Lonnie's convinced they're spies from the deep state," Moira says. He calls them Agent X and Agent Y now.

"They have secret meetings with Dr. Natas at night," Ox says. "And the three of them were gone all last weekend."

Lucie keeps trying to explain that it's all because of the investment company, Sibylla.

"Sounds like C-I-A to me," Ox says.

"No, it doesn't," Lucie says.

10:44 a.m.

In the art classroom, Mr. Silvenus sets her up on a stool and shows her how to feed the carded wool into the spinning wheel, but Frankie doesn't get it. She must've done this thousands of times in her old lives, so why isn't spinning coming back to her like swimming and cursive? Maybe she's too distracted. Or uncoordinated.

11:51 a.m.

As they heat up lunch, the counselors talk about the spirits. Scaredy Cat haunts the Mothership, while Nessie is still making the lake so freezing cold that they can't swim. A third one grazes with the sheep. They call him Dags.

"The flock seem totally cool with Dags, but Argus won't get near the sheep when the spirit is there," Lucie says.

"Ox won't, either," Efrat says.

"Ay, I'm not afraid of some woolly ghost, mate," Ox says.

As she carries a stack of plates to the buffet table, Frankie wonders if it could be the spirit of the sheep that died, and thinks again about what Dr. Natas did to it.

I probably shouldn't make so much fun of him.

"You need to teach us how to catch them," Efrat tells her.

Frankie says okay. "But what time?"

"At four," Efrat says. "When the Listeners go behind the veil."

"I can't. I'm, uh . . . ," Frankie pauses, "going behind the veil, too."

"What?" Ox says, slamming a tray of glasses down onto the table. "You run off for ten days and instead of getting suspended, you get bloody *promoted*? That's not fair."

Frankie doesn't know what to say, but Efrat answers for her.

"She is a more powerful channeler than the rest of us combined," Efrat says. "Who else would they have join? You? Your rugbyballing skills don't matter here."

"You know it's just called *rugby*," Ox mutters.

1:23 p.m.

Moira's been angling to pull Frankie aside all day, and finally succeeds as they clean up lunch. She needs to tell Frankie some news. *Important* news.

"Ox and I are . . . talking."

"Why on earth would you do that?"

This is not the reaction Moira was looking for but she blows past it, and now Frankie has to hear about how cute Oxnard is and somehow not throw up in her mouth. She wishes she was back in one of her past lives. Even the last days of Pompeii had to be better than hearing about Ox's six-pack.

"Can you *please* stop, Moira," Frankie says. "I seriously just ate."

On the plus side, at least Moira is no longer crushing on Lucie.

3:27 p.m.

Dr. Natas hands Ek the keys to the van along with cash to buy the counselors pizza in Demetria, the town on the other side of Proserpina.

"When do you want us back?" Ek says.

"Anytime after eight o'clock will do fine," Dr. Natas says.

Even though she's missing the outing to participate in a literally life-defining event, Frankie still has serious FOMO. A road trip *and* pizza.

"Can you bring me back a slice?"

Ek smiles. "Of course!"

4:04 p.m.

Finally. It's about to happen. Standing in the hallway-like anteroom of the crypt, Frankie and Mr. Silvenus can hear the Listeners through the door, snapping and chanting. She's never been down here before. Well, she *has*, but her past-life memories of the place only make it freakier.

"Untie your hair," Mr. Silvenus says.

"What? Why?"

"In Roman religious ceremonies, knots are prohibited. They're associated with spells and black magic. Take off your shoes, too," he says, pointing down. "Laces."

"You're no fun to get ready with," Frankie says as she kicks off her shoes. She pulls a foot up to her nose.

"What are you doing?" Mr. Silvenus says.

"Making sure my socks aren't smelly."

"They are."

Frankie pulls them off, too, and blindly attempts to style her loose hair. Even without a mirror she knows it's not going well.

"Stop fussing. You're putting on a hood," Mr. Silvenus says, holding up a velvet robe.

"So is this going to be like a quinceañera?" Frankie asks as she puts on the heavy cloak. "Or more gender reveal party?"

"I'm quite sure I don't know what either of those are."

The door to the inner chamber of the crypt opens. Frankie still can't get used to telekinesis. At least not when other people are doing it.

"Are you coming?" Frankie asks.

Mr. Silvenus shakes his head no. "I never cared much for circuses."

Frankie takes a deep breath, and steps over the threshold.

34
The Gift of Pythagoras

Dr. Natas looks at her. They're all looking at her.

Frankie stops.

The scene is the same as in her dream; the Listeners are assembled in a circle, levitating around a central fire on an altar. The long robes hang suspended from their crossed legs, the hems grazing the ground. Frankie looks from one Listener to the next, their hooded faces difficult to decipher in the flickering light. Only

Cadmus can she see clearly, as if his face were lit from within. Frankie's eyes meet his and he nods as if to say, *Walk forward.*

Dr. Natas snaps, the others join in, and Frankie steps into a memory of twenty-five years ago, when she was Mother presenting young Natas, the Listeners snapping then like now.

Cadmus was there, and Lonnie and his wives; the rest of the attendees were different. She sees Karl and Nasrat, but where's Fred? *Fred's dead.* Who even *was* Fred? She has a terrible feeling about him.

The Listeners begin to chant again, whether in the past or present or both she isn't sure. A drop of water falling on her forehead brings Frankie fully into the now, the cold wetness sliding down the bridge of her nose. Then, another memory snaps into place, of an even earlier ceremony, when Mother was introduced, and everyone was different. A strikingly handsome man draws her attention, his dark skin and long black hair a stark contrast to the others. The Founder must have been the same age then that Dr. Natas is now. And the way Ramakrishna was looking at her—the way Natas *is* looking at her—is also the same. Like a priest about to make a sacrifice.

The knife. In the present, Frankie looks for the knife and finds it on the altar lying next to a jewelry box—and three skulls. All of them are human.

Is one of the skulls mine?

She thinks about it.

They're all mine.

Is it too late to run?

Frankie's not ready for this. They said it themselves—she never comes back this fast. What was she *thinking*? She can't catch her breath. Her heart races. The space around her contracts. And that knife, it's now floating in front of Dr. Natas, the polished blade catching glints of flame.

How many times has she done this? Does this happen every life? She knows the answer: It doesn't. Frankie has lived entire lives in which she chose to have nothing to do with this, when she ran away and forgot her pasts and avoided ever speaking to him. *Him.* She doesn't even have a real name for him, because the names are incidental. Natas. Ramakrishna. Valerius. *Valerius* was the name she first knew him by, that Luna knew him by.

Frankie isn't frozen, or trapped. She could run, she *should* run, but it's that thing where you don't want to embarrass yourself in front of a room full of people, so you do what they expect of you even when you know that's never a good reason to do anything.

Dr. Natas unfolds his legs down from their levitating position, plucks the knife out of the air, and walks over to her. He takes Frankie by the hand and leads her to the altar. She looks down at the skulls. One of them is a brighter color of bone than the others. That skull must be Mother's.

"You, who have lived a thousand lives."

Dr. Natas brushes the hair away from her neck.

"You, who have died a thousand deaths."

He raises the knife.

"You, who have been granted the gift of Pythagoras."

He cuts a lock of her hair.

"Let us receive the blessing of your awakening, the blessing of . . . your reincarnation."

Dr. Natas tosses her hair onto the altar's fire. It shrivels; the smell is repulsive. She'll never forget that smell.

"Frances," he says.

Frankie looks up. She can feel everyone looking at her. Her heart thumps.

"Frances," he repeats. "It is time."

The top of the jewelry box opens, revealing the amulet. Link by link, the necklace rises from the box, the tiger's-eye staring at her. Back when she found it in Dr. Natas's apartment, her mind was lifting it; whether now Dr. Natas is doing it or all the Listeners collectively are, Frankie isn't sure, but again the chain attaches itself around her neck, its clasp connecting right where Natas sliced off the lock of hair.

For the first time, Frankie catches sight of Wilma. She's smiling. Not her demonic little fang smile, but the big, full smile of someone who can't contain their pleasure.

Dr. Natas lowers his hood, then Frankie's; he kisses her on each cheek, then the forehead, and says:

"Welcome back, Mother."

35

The Return of Mother

Frankie is disoriented. Words swirl around her.

"I knew it! I knew you'd come back!"

"Her eyes! I told you she had Mother's eyes!"

"I knew Frances was the one!"

The one—they kept calling her *the one*. Like her mother called Dr. Natas.

In the anteroom, Frankie hangs her cloak on a hook and feels a hand take hold of hers, to lead her up the stairs.

"How are you?" Wilma asks, squeezing her fingers. "How do you feel?"

"Happy," Frankie says.

But "happy" doesn't begin to describe the surge of joy she's feeling. Or the love. *Love* is the most palpable emotion inside the soaring, central space of Chapel. These sweet, aging hippies might be awed by the Founder, but they love Mother.

The table is set, the buffet steaming; the other counselors prepared the meal before they left to get pizza. In contrast to the ceremony, the dinner is decidedly non-freaky, almost like a birthday party.

Without the other counselors—and without Mr. Silvenus's place cards—everyone sits where they want. Frankie has Cadmus on one side of her, Wilma on the other. Eeva serves her a plate of food while Lonnie pours her something to drink.

Diana hits him on the arm.

"You can't give her wine!" Diana says in her hard-of-hearing, shouty voice.

"What do you mean?" Lonnie says. "Mother always drank wine."

"But she's *fourteen*!"

Meanwhile, Frankie has her wrist grabbed from across the table. "Do you remember Minnesota?" Penny asks.

Minnesota? Not at all.

"Hennepin Avenue," Penny says. "You must remember what happened at the donut shop."

"Oh, yeah, *Hennepin*," Frankie says, doing the pretend-you-remember thing. Then she deflects, asking if Penny remembers that time in the Pine Barrens—the flat tire, the ripped tent, the mosquitoes. Mother got the worst welts from mosquitoes.

"The Pine Barrens!" Penny says, beaming. She turns to Lonnie. "Can you believe Mother remembers that trip?"

"Do you *really* remember the Pine Barrens?" Wilma whispers into her ear.

"Totally," Frankie says, covering her mouth.

The memories stream back—nice ones now. Her head spins; Frankie feels like she *is* drinking wine. Unfortunately, none of these memories are the ones the Listeners want her to talk about.

"When I was a student here, I took your elective on psychology," Eeva says. "Do you remember my term paper?"

"Of course I do," Frankie lies. She doesn't remember Eeva even a little. Who Frankie does remember—who she's shocked to remember—is Agent Y. Not as a Listener or a student, and not even from this country.

"Tokyo." Frankie leans toward him across the table. "The bank. You set up all the accounts."

Agent Y's face goes red. "I didn't think you'd recall," he sheepishly says.

Completing the birthday party vibe, Diana serves a cake after dinner. WELCOME BACK MOTHER is written in icing. The only thing missing is candles to blow out.

As the others hug her good night after dessert and head back to their rooms, Cadmus sits in silence, waiting, as he had the whole meal. When it's only the two of them and Wilma, Cadmus rises out of his chair into a standing position, the tips of his shoes just brushing the floor, and locks his gaze onto hers. His eyes shine brighter than ever, more blue than gray. He looks like some kind of angel, if angels were old. And who's to say they aren't?

"Mother," he says, taking her hands into his. *"There will be no goodbye."*

He speaks the phrase with such purpose that it sounds like a coded message, like she will know what it means. Cadmus must see in her face that she has no idea, because he tilts his head in a gesture of disappointment.

Suddenly, Frankie feels overwhelmed by impostor syndrome. She searches for something—*anything*—to say to him, to make this the moment he wants it to be, that he's waited sixteen years to happen, but Frankie is drawing a blank. She can't remember him any better than Eeva.

Then, the memory of a boy pops into her head. A young boy, curled up in his bed. Mother pulls a book from a shelf and asks Cadmus, "Do you want this one?"

The painful ache of nostalgia fills her soul as she relives showing him the cover. Here, in Chapel, she looks up into the blue-gray eyes of Cadmus, an elder angel floating in front of her, and repeats the same words she said then.

"You're my own little bull," she says. "My Ferdinand."

Which is the weirdest thing a teenage girl ever said to an old man, but Frankie had no choice. It's like her Mother-self has taken over, and Frankie is sitting in the back seat of her own body.

"He had a favorite spot out in the pasture," she reads from memory, *"under a cork tree."*

Hearing the words, Cadmus collapses into her arms, no longer able to keep himself afloat. He sobs, and Frankie struggles to hold him up.

※

Wilma and Frankie sit out on the front steps of the Mothership, having just helped Cadmus to bed. They're eating cold pizza from the box Ek brought back.

"So you're really her, huh?" Wilma says, chewing.

"You already knew that," Frankie says.

"But I didn't actually believe it."

Frankie takes a bite. "Me neither," she says. In fact, she's still not sure she does.

Donut shops in Minnesota, former students, and *no goodbye*s. How could she not remember any of it?

"I feel like a fraud."

"A fraud?" Wilma gives Frankie her sideways look. "The fact that you remember my grandfather and the others at all is a miracle," Wilma says, putting down the pizza. "It's not about *you*, it's about them. They get to talk to someone who died. Someone they loved has come back to life."

Frankie says, "I don't think I've ever heard you say something serious before."

"Well, I've never watched someone get reincarnated before." Wilma picks back up her slice. "God, I love cold pizza."

"Who doesn't?" Frankie says, and takes another bite.

36

Spinning

There's something soothing about the spinning wheel, the way it glides when you press your foot down on the pedal. Frankie feels like that girl in Rumpelstiltskin.

The way Mr. Silvenus talks while they spin is also comforting.

"As you work, please consider the powerful symbolism of the art in which you partake. To the Romans, destiny lay in the hands of three spinners: Nona, who spun human life; Decima, who measured its span; and Morta, who cut the thread, determining life's end. *Our* end." The Latin teacher wanders the room like he's speaking to them one at a time. "Cultures that see life and death in less linear terms find their symbol not in the thread but in the spinning wheel itself. For them, the steady turn of the wheel represents the endless cycling of a soul's rebirth. Reincarnation!"

Mr. Silvenus looks right at Frankie when he says *reincarnation*. Could he be any more obvious? None of the counselors pick up on it, though. Except her brother.

Frankie has to keep reminding herself that the other kids have no idea she's Mother. They're having enough trouble getting their head wrapped around Frankie now being one of the Listeners.

"Do we have to, like, do stuff for you?" Moira asked yesterday.

"No," Frankie said. "Definitely not."

She also has to remind herself that the Listeners *do* know she's Mother.

Ox gets up from his spinning wheel.

"What are you doing, Mr. Oxnard?" Mr. Silvenus says.

"Break time, mate," Ox says, pointing at the clock above the door.

"You indicate the clock, and yet you fail to comprehend that you have to wait until the long hand reaches the twelve for the hour to be struck," Mr. Silvenus says. "I do apologize if such old-fashioned timekeeping devices confound you."

Ox cuts out early every night at cleanup, too.

With a dramatic sigh he sits back down and lazily presses the pedal, spinning the wheel without even feeding it any wool.

He is such a jerk.

Five minutes later, they're all on break. The Listeners stay in the art room while the kids gather around the water fountain in the hall. Cadmus isn't here for the second day in a row and Frankie's afraid that the reincarnation ceremony was too much for him. Or worse—that he was so disappointed, he doesn't want to see her again.

"Not at all," Wilma whispers. "He thinks you're exactly like Mother. It's the heat."

On his turn at the fountain, Ox lets the water run as he turns back to Frankie.

"So now that you're behind the veil," he says, pausing to take a sip, "you can tell us what goes on down there."

"Stop worrying about places you don't belong," Efrat says.

Frankie tells them it's no big deal. "Mostly, Dr. Natas just gives a talk like he does during the school year. The Listeners listen, and that's it."

Except that what he's talking about is way more fascinating than any of his Sunday sermons. Yesterday, Dr. Natas spoke about his past life as an Incan tax collector and how he kept his accounts using a spreadsheet-like system of strings and knots called a *quipu*. Afterward, they did a long meditation that bored Frankie, but Dr. Natas promised that today would be something "interesting."

Back at their wheels, spinning, Ox won't let the veil thing drop.

"If it's no big deal," he says, "then why can't *we*—"

"Oh my god!" Moira yells, jumping up from her stool and knocking over her spinning wheel. "What *is* that?!"

A spirit passes through Moira's thread, spooking everyone, and races out the open window.

"Well, at least it's finally air-conditioned in here!" Lonnie says.

This is a new spirit, everyone agrees. The first to show up in weeks.

Since I left, Frankie thinks. Could it possibly be a coincidence? The horrible feeling that it's not returns—that *she's* responsible for these things getting out of the Oblivion.

"Now will you teach us how to catch them?" Efrat says.

Frankie sighs.

"Start collecting plastic bottles," she says.

37

Alarming

"**My own body** was rotting. The lesions on my skin marked me as one to be shunned by society."

He suffered from leprosy; he was despised. Down in the crypt, Dr. Natas re-creates a life he led in ancient Mesopotamia.

"I never allowed my body to become a prison, for I knew this too would pass. That one day my soul would be liberated."

Snapping.

The charred black skull of the Founder rises up from the altar and floats into the outstretched palm of Dr. Natas. He looks into its eye sockets.

"These dark, gaping voids once housed the eyes out of which I myself saw the world. It is important to gaze upon a vessel such as this and remember," he says. "Remember that this is all our bodies ever are. A shell."

"A *shell*," Lonnie says.

"A *shell*," they all say.

Frankie mouths the words. They did this same ritual yesterday.

"Today, we will attempt to tempo*rarily* free ourselves from our shells," Dr. Natas says, looking to each of the Listeners in turn. "To separate soul from body."

Alarm bells go off in Frankie's head and she shoots a *what-is-he-talking-about* look to Wilma, but her focus is straight ahead.

"Soften your gaze and breathe deeply . . ."

Frankie reluctantly follows the body scan Dr. Natas guides them through. Beginning with the extremities—the hair and fingernails, the skin—he leads them inward, to their muscles and bones, to the blood flowing through their veins, and finally to the soul.

He actually says the word—"soul"—but how can you *feel* your soul?

Asking them to receive their deepest breath of the day, Dr. Natas leads them in a single chanting exhale of:

"Ohmmm..."

Even after the breath is spent and the chant ended, their bodies continue to hum. Frankie can feel a vibration inside of her, a quivering, of two forces repelling each other. Is one of *these* her soul?

Remember Rule One, Dr. Natas says, a whisper inside their minds. *If you separate, resist the temptation to enter the Oblivion.*

Rule One? No one said anything about a Rule One! And what does he mean, *enter the Oblivion*? Is that really even a possibility right now? More alarm bells.

Breaking Rule One isn't going to be a problem, however, because none of the Listeners manage to separate. Apparently, souls tend to stay pretty stubbornly attached to their bodies.

Now that they've tried and failed, Frankie's alarm gives way to disappointment.

"Don't worry, we've got the rest of the week to go splitsville," Lonnie says in the anteroom, telekinetically returning his cloak to its hook while fetching his shoes. The Listeners are all doing it, and what three days ago felt magical now feels like waiting for the other bus passengers to get their luggage from the overhead rack.

"I've never managed to break free," Eeva cheerily tells Frankie as they walk upstairs. "I'm hoping with you here, it will finally happen for me."

"Why with me here?"

"Because we get strength from each other, like with levitating," she says. "I sure hope Cadmus can come tomorrow. With the two of you *and* Dr. Natas, our souls should pop right out!"

Are all Finnish people this positive?

38

Becomes the Teacher

Pine-Sol, Mr. Clean, Clorox. Plastic bottles line the edge of the flagstone patio in front of Chapel.

"Okay, mate, we got 'em," Ox says. "Now what?"

"Practice," Frankie says, pouring a small puddle of water from a cup onto one of the smooth rectangular stones of the terrace. "If you can will the water into a bottle, you can catch a spirit."

The sisters did this same drill with her, except they didn't explain why. Frankie aims to be a better teacher.

"Start by focusing on a single bead," Frankie says. "Get the feel of moving the water around, then try pulling it up the side of the bottle."

Efrat gets the hang of it instantly, with Ek not far behind. The others are hopeless.

A weak breeze could move this water better than these three, Frankie finds herself thinking as she watches. She begins to understand why Not-Estelle would get so frustrated with her.

Moira gives up and Ox slams a horn into a wall. "This is bloody impossible!" he says.

"But Efrat and Ek just did it," Lucie says.

"Why don't you guys work as a team?" Frankie suggests to the three of them. "Choose one drop, and all focus on it together."

Combining their efforts, they manage to roll a bead of water as far as the Clorox bottle, but fail to draw it up the side. It's pathetic to watch the one little drop struggle.

"Are you even trying?" Lucie says to Ox.

"Trying? *I'm* the one who moved it!" He hooks a thumb at Moira. "She's the one holding us back, mate."

"Hey, I'm trying, too!" Moira says.

"The drop just evaporated," Efrat says.

"Are any of you going to put out the food?" Mr. Silvenus calls from the doorway of Chapel. "The Listeners are arriving, and they're hungry. As am I."

"Let's go set up dinner, so these guys can keep practicing," Ek says to Efrat and Frankie.

The trays are heated and the salad is getting dressed when Moira comes bouncing in.

"Come on, come on! You have to see."

Frankie watches the water climb up the side of the bottle, like beads of condensation rolling in reverse. "Very good," she tells them.

"So we can trap spirits now?" Lucie says, a big goofy smile reaching from horn to horn.

"It's a start," Frankie says.

"Let's go bloody hunting!" Ox says.

"Frankie already told us that isn't how it works," Efrat says.

"Actually," Frankie says, "I might've been wrong about that."

39
Mind Mapping

Putting Scaredy Cat into the bottle is like getting her old cat into the pet carrier. Ella always hid under the bed and would desperately grip the floor with her claws, scraping the wood as Frankie dragged her out. The only difference with Scaredy is that, instead of a bed, Frankie finds the shadow cat crouching under the Victorian sofa in the sitting room of the Mothership.

Having shown them how it's done, Frankie gives the other counselors a chance to capture the next spirit.

It doesn't go as well.

First, Ox won't get within a hundred feet of Dags, who's peacefully grazing alongside the living sheep in the meadow.

"He's the least menacing spirit ever," Frankie says. "How can you be afraid of him?"

"I'm not afraid, mate." He points at his bare shins below his shorts. "It's the stinging nettles."

Yeah, right.

Now Efrat insists on trying to capture the spirit alone, but when she tries to grab Dags, he races away and Frankie has to finish the job. Trying to be sympathetic, Frankie tells her how badly she did her first couple of times out, to which Efrat replies, "Well, *I* would have caught him if you let me."

Again: *Yeah, right.*

What's crazy about all this is that Frankie *can* hunt spirits now. She already knew she didn't have to see the shadows to grab them, but now she can locate them anywhere inside the walls.

Frankie realized the ability first with people, like how she could "see" Moira after they levitated together no matter where she was, like she can with everyone now. Maybe it's what Estelle calls an aura. Places have them, too, and referencing spirit against location is how Frankie tracked down Scaredy Cat and Dags.

But it's not working with Nessie.

"She's somewhere in the lake," Moira says, pointing.

"Yeah, I got that," Frankie says.

"Maybe your mind-map-GPS powers don't work under the water," Lucie says. "Like how there's no cell phone signal inside the walls."

The water isn't the problem, though; the Boathouse is. The sense of dread the ruins give off is so strong it overwhelms everything around it, like when green curry is so spicy you can't tell what kind of vegetables you're even eating.

As disappointed as everyone is, they decide to give up and go play Ping-Pong.

40
Ghost Season

Not being able to find Nessie isn't the only source of frustration. Behind the veil, no one's able to separate. What makes it more annoying is that now Frankie can *feel* her soul, it just has no interest in going anywhere.

As the Listeners put their socks and shoes back on, Frankie asks Wilma if she wants to go spirit catching.

"It's way more satisfying than this."

They trapped three shadows yesterday, including the one from the spinning wheel.

Wilma shakes her head no. "I kind of like having the spirits around," she says. "Besides, I need to spend time with Grandpa."

Cadmus still hasn't come out of their room.

"Are you sure he's okay?" Frankie asks.

Wilma nods. "It's the heat."

In Bob's shed, Moira thinks the heat might have something to do with the spirits, too.

"Maybe they're seasonal," she says. "Like fireflies."

"Ghosts don't have seasons," Ox says.

"How do you know?" Efrat says. "Last year, it was also summer when they appeared."

Frankie likes the seasonal explanation better than it being her fault. Whatever the cause, the spirits keep coming. The two they caught today were so new, they didn't even have time to name them.

The counselors go down to the lake again, but it's the same problem as before. All Frankie can do is scour the water for Nessie with her eyes like the rest of the kids.

"We have to find her," Moira says. "I really wanna be able to swim again."

"Oh, you want to go swimming, do you?" Ox says to Moira.

"No no no!" Moira says as Ox picks her up and takes a step into the lake.

Frankie really can't handle the flirting with these two.

"Guys, look!" Lucie says, pointing out into the lake. "Do you see that? Ice!"

Ox drops Moira.

"Hey!" she says, quickly hopping out of the cold water.

"It *does* look like a patch of ice," Ek says, squinting.

"Even if Nessie's under there, how are we going to catch her?" Frankie says. "It's too far from shore."

For once, Ox has a good idea.

"I don't think this is meant for six people," Ek says, gripping either side of the teetering rowboat.

"It's fine, mate," Ox says, pushing an oar against a rock and launching them.

As Oxnard rows, the boat steadies out. Gliding on top of the still, chilly water is like entering the walk-in cooler of the Wagon Wheel.

"Over there." Lucie points. "The water's rippling."

As they turn to look, a shadow slowly emerges from the lake, and keeps emerging. Frankie has never seen a spirit anywhere near this size. Maybe this *is* the Loch Ness Monster.

"Get the bottle, get the bottle!" Ox says.

"Here," Moira says, fumbling the top.

"Nessie's on the move!"

Unfortunately, all the combined channeling powers of the counselors don't much bother Nessie. The shadow monster keeps surfacing and disappearing, swimming as calmly as a dolphin. Then she's just gone. The entire lake is still.

"They're not all going to be as easy as Scaredy Cat," Frankie says.

With Ek in the back holding an oar in the water as a rudder, Ox rows to turn the boat around.

Moira sighs loudly. "I really thought we had her this time."

As Moira says "time," the boat rises out of the water. *Are we levitating?* No. Nessie is lifting the rowboat. And then she drops it.

The boat flips over as it falls, the kids screaming and shouting. Except for Frankie, plunging underwater.

Panic seizes her. She inhales a mouthful of lake water and coughs it out as she surfaces, flailing. Then she remembers: *I can swim.*

"It's so cold, guys!" Ek says, leading the others to shore.

"Guys, I think Nessie's following us!" Moira yells, paddling and kicking frantically.

Forget swimming, Frankie decides. She floats to her back, flips over onto her elbows and knees, pushes herself up and starts running across the surface of the lake. Water splashes up like she's stomping through puddles.

"Hey, sis! Help *us* do that!"

"Yeah, mate!" Ox yells. "Gives us a boost!"

"Sorry, guys," Frankie hollers back. "You're on your own!"

41

Harvesting

On the other side of the sheepfold from the school, rows of vegetables and flowers climb the rolling hill that leads to the north wall. At the base of the hill, in front of a wooden gardening shed, Bob hands out baskets to the Listeners.

"Kale," he says to Lonnie.

"Chatty as ever, eh, Bob?" Lonnie says, looking up into the black eyeballs of the giant deem.

In addition to being the groundskeeper, Bob runs the school's farming club. Students grow seedlings in the greenhouse which they transplant to the fields, with the idea that the produce go to a food pantry in Demetria.

Lonnie joins the other Listeners, already harvesting the vegetable beds. In the shade at the edge of the woods, Penny sits with Cadmus. This is the first time anyone other than Wilma has seen him since the beginning of the week.

"How are you, Mother?" Cadmus says when Frankie comes over to say hello. It's jarring; the other Listeners only call her that behind the veil. "I've been wanting to see you, but this heat . . ."

Diana keeps asking Cadmus how he's feeling, and it clearly embarrasses him. He looks so weak, slumped down in a folding chair, wearing boxy sunglasses and a baseball cap pulled low, his pale face glistening with dots of perspiration. Should he really be out here?

Bob is now handing out harvesting assignments to the kids, and Wilma and Frankie walk over to join.

"Is your grandpa going behind the veil today?" Frankie asks.

She nods.

Eeva will be happy. Since it's Friday, today is their final opportunity to separate. Dr. Natas has already told them they'll be doing something different next week.

"Have *you* ever separated before?" Frankie whispers.

Fang smile.

"I'll take that as a yes."

"String beans," Bob says to Moira, handing her a basket with a pair of scissors.

"I'm sick," Moira says, sniffling. "I think I got hypothermia in the lake last night."

Bob blinks at her like she's speaking a foreign language. Then he drops a pair of clippers into a pail and hands it to Wilma, and does the same with Frankie.

"Sunflowers," he says.

The two girls walk between colorful beds of wildflowers, shears rattling in their metal buckets. On the crest of the hill beyond, rows of sunflowers stand tall, their heads facing the morning sun.

As they go, Frankie talks about her latest recovered memory, from the year that Mother and two of the Listeners spent in Paris, studying at the Sorbonne. "I could see the Eiffel Tower from my room! Isn't that crazy?" Wilma doesn't respond and Frankie worries she's coming off braggy, but is Wilma listening? She won't even look at her.

"Why are you acting weird?" Frankie says as they reach the first row of sunflowers. "Weirder than usual, I mean."

Wilma unclips the lock on her shears and turns away from Frankie toward the sunflowers. They're so much taller than her.

"When you remember the other Listeners," Wilma says, looking up at a drooping flower head, "is one of them ever my mom?"

"Oh."

Frankie wishes she could take back what she just said.

"Yeah, I do," Frankie says. "From when she was a little girl, helping me in the kitchen of my apartment. I was at the sink, washing dishes, and she was drying them with a blue-checked towel. She had to climb onto a chair to put the plates in the cabinets."

"For real?"

"For real."

Frankie can't tell if her Mother-self is taking over again, or if the memory is so vivid it only feels like she is.

Wilma holds the sunflower as high as she can reach and cuts the stalk off right below her hand. She puts the sunflower head in the bucket.

"How old were you?" Frankie says. "When she died."

Wilma turns her back to Frankie again, grabbing another sunflower stem.

"If you don't want to talk about it . . . ," Frankie says.

"I was eight."

Snip.

Frankie says, "How long had she been sick?"

"I never remember her not being sick." Wilma stares at the head of the sunflower she just cut. "She would get better. Then not be better. Then she died."

Wilma drops the head in the bucket.

Frankie suddenly imagines her own mom getting sick and dying and feels like bursting into tears. Why was Frankie so mad at her anyway? What did it really matter, that Mom lied about how she was born? She was lucky to still have a mom.

"I found out I'm adopted," Frankie says.

She hadn't told anyone. Not even Lucie.

Wilma turns back to Frankie with that look in her eye—the slightly evil one.

"*You* adopted my grandfather."

This isn't the reaction Frankie was expecting. "I don't think Mother legally adopted him," she says.

"But Grandpa thinks of you as his mother, which makes you *my* great-grandmother," Wilma says, fangs out. "Can I call you *gam-gam*?"

Frankie unlocks her shears, springing open their jaws.

"Honest to god, Wilma, you really are the weirdest person ever."

She tries, but Frankie can't keep from smiling.

42

Unyoke the Yolk

Lonnie is the only one of the Listeners who dares to joke with Dr. Natas, but inside the crypt, even he is solemn. The newcomers and old-timers alike act as if every word the man utters is a revelation, like he's more than just a man. Having Cadmus back behind the veil, Frankie realizes that there's someone else the Listeners are in awe of.

Hovering just above the steps, Cadmus glides down the stairwell, and even though they all channel to change clothes, there's something more elegant about the way he does it, as if a dozen hands were attending to him, removing his hat and sunglasses, untying his shoes, smoothing the cloak.

In the crypt itself, the energy crackles with him there, like the buzz you get on a sleepover after the parents tell you not to stay up too late and the bedroom door closes and there's a giddy sense of release.

Release. The body scan is only just beginning and already Frankie feels it—her soul releasing. She never came close to separating before, she now realizes. Before, her soul felt like an object to seize; now, she *is* her soul, and it's the rest of her body that's the object. Leaving it takes no effort. In fact, she's already gone.

Frankie is *outside* of her body.

Disoriented, Frankie can't understand what's happening, or how to control her movement. She floats, but it's nothing like levitation. Levitating is a struggle against the weight of your body; even when others do the lifting, gravity still pulls at you. This is true weightlessness. Frankie feels as if she could float away forever, like a runaway balloon.

Then she hits up against something. The ceiling. Right—a spirit can't go through walls.

I can't believe I'm a spirit!

Frankie becomes aware of the other Listeners hovering around her. They look like the shadows she's captured, with one difference: In each of their faces, Frankie can see flickering hints of who they are—and who they used to be. Penny is simultaneously her present wrinkled self and the hippie girl from Mother's memories and a glamorous middle-aged actress. And Eeva, with the dyed-purple hair that covers her face—of course Eeva! Frankie says, *I remember you! You sat up front and always asked such smart questions. I knew you'd amount to something.* But Eeva can't hear her, either because Frankie isn't really speaking or because Eeva is so ecstatic to have finally separated that she's oblivious.

Frankie looks down at her body to make sure that it's still there, that she can return if she wants to. It's hard to find herself;

Frankie's never seen her body from the outside before. When she does, it appears as lifeless and empty as the skulls and way more grotesque, a sack of skin holding flesh and bones.

*Why would I want to go back to **that**?*

Taking in her surroundings, Frankie becomes aware of a soft glow. Was it there before? Is it always there? The light suffuses the entire space, and Frankie feels drawn to submerge herself into the deepest part of it, like she would a warm bath.

Resist the light.

The voice comes from inside her head.

Remember Rule One. We must all resist the light.

The voice of Dr. Natas shakes Frankie out of whatever trance she was in. Her mind clears like ears popping on a descent, allowing her to remember. *That's the Oblivion,* she thinks. *I was so young, the first time I went inside of it.* When Luna did.

Luna went in *a lot*.

Frankie doesn't need to resist it—she wants no part of entering the light. Suddenly feeling unmoored and adrift, Frankie hurtles across the room like one of those desperate shadows she chased, hardly understanding her soul is reentering her body even as the two merge. Immediately, she feels the air on her skin, the dryness in her mouth, and an ache in her belly that must be hunger.

The map inside her mind is back, too, and she senses the other Listeners around her, also returned to their bodies. Except for one—Eeva. Where is she?

There. Dissolving into the light. Alarm bells go off again, this time violently, as she realizes: *Eeva is entering the Oblivion.*

Like any other spirit she's caught, Frankie grabs ahold of Eeva with her mind. Surprised, Eeva doesn't even think to resist, and

Frankie easily sends her spiraling down into her body, which—unlike a plastic bottle—seals itself.

Eeva's eyes pop open. She sucks in a breath and says, "Oh!"

The other Listeners laugh. Except for Frankie. Her heart pounds. Why won't it stop pounding?

43
Rule One

"**That was incredible!**" Eeva says. "Incredible!"

"We did kinda just squirt right out, didn't we?" Lonnie chuckles, grabbing a sneaker out of the air and slipping it on. "Like the old days."

"You can thank this man," Penny says, squeezing Cadmus's upper arm.

Wilma's grandfather is invigorated, nothing like the person melting in the field this morning. But Penny is more different still. She's suddenly lucid, her mind like a dirty windshield that's been wiped clean.

The Mysterions are also transformed. They're even speaking.

"I can't believe it," X says, still stunned. "We did it. We really did it."

"I thought separating was a deeper state of meditation," Y says. "But we *actually* went outside of our bodies."

Lonnie slaps them on their backs, no longer concerned that they're neo-fascist secret agents.

"Let's go eat! Nothing makes you hungrier than a good out-of-body experience!"

Raucous laughter and a cacophony of chatter explode down the narrow staircase as the Listeners file up out of the crypt. On the bottom step, Wilma turns back to Frankie.

"You coming?"

"In a minute," Frankie says.

Wilma shrugs and follows the others up, leaving Frankie and Dr. Natas alone.

"Is there something?" Dr. Natas says.

He knows there's something.

"How close was Eeva to entering the Oblivion just now?"

"Close?" Dr. Natas says. "She was already inside the Oblivion."

"Wait—seriously?" Frankie says, shocked. "Why are you having us separate if it's so easy?"

"No one gets lost on the edge of a forest," Dr. Natas says.

"What does *that* mean?"

"That the fringes of the Oblivion hold no danger," he says, removing his cloak. "Besides, you were there to rescue Eeva if she went any further. Shepherding lost souls back from the Oblivion has always been your job." Dr. Natas turns to go up the stairs, but Frankie stops him.

"What would have happened to Eeva if she kept going?"

"The same thing that happens to every soul inside the Oblivion," Dr. Natas says. "She would begin to forget."

"Forget?"

"The Oblivion is the forgetting, the place where a soul gets washed clean of its memory, so it can enter a new body."

"That's how reincarnation works?"

Dr. Natas nods.

First off, *whoa*. But: "Does that mean you can get reincarnated while you're still alive?"

"Reincarnation is not instantaneous, but a process. You should know," Dr. Natas says. "Luna used to roam the Oblivion for hours at a time."

"But if someone stays in long enough for their memories to be wiped out, what happens to their body?"

"Why, it dies, of course."

That's not good.

"And until it dies," Frankie asks, "the body just sits there, empty?"

"A body is never empty for long," Dr. Natas says. "Nature abhors a vacuum."

Frankie doesn't understand.

"Vacated bodies get inhabited by spirits," Dr. Natas says.

"You mean, like, *possessed*?"

Dr. Natas shakes his head no. "The body rejects the foreign soul and expels it out to the other side," he says. "This side."

"So *that's* how spirits escape the Oblivion?" Frankie says.

"That is one way," he says. "A body devoid of a soul is a portal between the two realms."

"That must be what's happening!" Frankie says. "Someone's been going inside the Oblivion and leaving the door open."

"If this week showed you nothing else, it should be how difficult it is to separate," Dr. Natas says in his most patronizing voice. "The entire group of Listeners working together were necessary to accomplish the task even once."

"But the sisters somehow did it. Just the two of them."

"And that is why we must make sure they stay where they are," Dr. Natas says. "Now, if you will allow me, I would like to go eat something. Separating makes me hungry as well."

"You don't need anyone's help to separate, do you?" Frankie says, stopping him at the foot of the stairs. "Maybe the spirits are exiting through *your* body."

"My dear Frances," Dr. Natas says, "when I leave a room, I know how to shut the door."

44

Ghost Story

The Lay's, or *the Doritos?* That's the eternal question. Since there's no use taking a risk, she grabs both. And some Twinkies, too.

Unless you're really craving empty calories, shopping at the O-K Kwik Mart is a grim experience. It's been nine months since the Scream Queen attack and the front windows are still covered in plywood, and not even nice plywood. Aren't they ever going to replace them?

In the rear soda aisle, Frankie gets a liter of A-Treat black cherry soda and bumps into a friend. Literally.

"Frankie?" Sylvie says.

"Oh, hey," Frankie says. "What are you doing here?"

"Ran outta the secret ingredient in the atomic burger sauce," Sylvie says, holding up a bottle of French's mustard. "Come back to the Wheel with me."

"Uh, your dad?" Frankie is convinced Mr. Zorn hates her. After all, it's Frankie's fault Sylvie drove to New Jersey on her learner's permit.

"I told you—he's mad at me, not you," Sylvie says. "He expects other people's kids to be runaways and losers, just not his own."

"That makes me feel *so* much better."

Now Frankie wants to go inside the Wagon Wheel even less. Instead, she puts the bag of snacks and soda into her backpack, slings it over her shoulder, and walks Sylvie to the corner. They say goodbye and Frankie heads back toward school, walking slowly, not only because she's dreading seeing the sisters but to get some alone time. She's had enough of the Listeners and way too much of the counselors. Efrat is getting on Frankie's nerves the most; she keeps insisting on catching spirits without any help and getting defensive when she fails.

The spirits have become a full-blown epidemic. They trapped five this morning, with Lonnie and Diana pitching in. Frankie thinks Dr. Natas could be lying about not letting them out—the one thing she remembers from all her past lives is not to trust him—but that doesn't answer why they only escape when *she* is at the Institute. It also only happens at night. Could the shadows be escaping through her body when she's asleep?

Feed Your Faith & Your Fears Will Starve

Her phone vibrates.

> **MISTRAL** DUDE! Whats wrong with you? You don't come say hi?

Frankie texts him a snarky reply but the message won't deliver; she's already out of signal range. How can that be? She's *at* the cell tower.

No bars appear as she walks, and her anxiety builds. Then she feels something—another spirit. She feels it *so* strongly. But how? She's still outside the walls.

Frankie arrives at the front gate.

THE PYTHAGOREAN INSTITUTE
EST. 1931

In front of the sign, a spirit sits on a large rock, like anyone might sit.

Frankie gets a shiver. Not because it's cold—it's not cold at all—but because it's so disturbing to see an escaped soul out here.

A car passes, startling Frankie. Does the driver sees what she's seeing? No. Because what driver would pay any attention to a shadow?

Frankie pulls the black cherry soda from her backpack. She hates to dump out the whole bottle to catch a spirit. And *this* spirit. It's just sitting there. Frankie sighs and twists the cap.

Sss.

With the sound of the soda, the shadow looks up. Frankie feels something more than a shiver—it's like a splinter of ice at the base of her spine. Because this spirit is different. Frankie can see it—see *her*. The spirit looks like how the Listeners did when they separated. Now a woman, now a girl; now in her teens, now in her thirties. Her hair is long and straight no matter the age, and she looks like she's trying to concentrate.

I think I'm lost.

How is the shadow *talking*? The voice is inside Frankie's head—like with Dr. Natas.

"Lost?" Frankie says out loud. Her heart skips a beat.

Do you know where we are?

Frankie looks around, unsure what to say, other than "Yeah." She pauses. "Do *you* know where we are?"

The shadow woman opens her mouth to say something, then closes it. She looks confused. Frankie's heart beats faster.

I was in the car, going to work. There was a text, from . . .

The woman looks back at Frankie, confusion overwhelmed by terror. She opens her mouth again, this time to scream.

The sound inside her head is so loud, Frankie winces in pain. Fleeing, the shadow races through the gate and gets swallowed in the darkness of the woods.

Blood still pulsing, Frankie cautiously walks over to where the spirit was sitting. She feels the rock. It's barely cold at all.

Frankie screws the cap back on the soda.

45

What She Doesn't Know

"It's **certainly been** a while," Not-Estelle says with a snort. An actual snort. "What's so important in your life that you can't visit us for weeks?"

Not-Estelle is angry with her when she comes and angry when she doesn't. At least Frankie finally knows why Not-Estelle hates her.

"Ooh, Twinkies!"

The O-K Kwik Mart bag crinkles as Estelle rummages through it.

Frankie rehearsed in her head what to say, but it's gone. She's too flustered. That ghost at the gate—that woman—she didn't even know she was dead.

POP. Estelle opens the Lay's. Not-Estelle talks, complaining, but Frankie's not listening. Finally, she blurts out what she needs to say.

"Look, I know why you guys treat me like you do. I know who I am." Frankie takes in a deep breath. "Who I *was*."

A thin, malicious smile comes to Not-Estelle's lips.

"We know you know," Estelle says, her mouth full of chips.

"You *do*?" Frankie says. "How?"

"Silvenus told us."

"Well, why didn't you say something when I walked in?" Frankie says. "Here I am sweating telling you guys."

"Poor you," Not-Estelle says, making a pretend sad face. "The person who's kept us trapped here for forty years under penalty of death had an uncomfortable sixty seconds."

As usual, her sister is more positive.

"How does it feel to know your true self, dear?" Estelle says. "Is it *so* exciting?"

Frankie doesn't know how to answer that. Especially with Not-Estelle looking like she might lunge at Frankie and strangle her.

"I'm not sure I have a true self," Frankie says. "Most of the time, I don't feel like I ever was Mother."

"Oh, isn't that convenient?" Not-Estelle says, now with a scoff instead of a snort. "I suppose you're going to say you don't 'feel' like it's your fault we're imprisoned."

"She's really not very much like Mother, you know," Estelle says, chewing. "She's such a sweet young girl."

"Oh, please, she's so much like Mother. Arrogant!"

"I'm arrogant?" Frankie says.

"No, dear," Estelle says, patting her back.

"Well, she's every bit as sarcastic."

"Mother was sarcastic?" Frankie says.

Maybe we're more alike than I thought.

"Their auras *are* identical," Estelle says, looking Frankie up and down like it's an undeniable fact. "But Mother would never have been so considerate as to buy us these lovely snacks."

"What does it matter?" Not-Estelle says. "Fault is fault, and there's only one way whoever this girl feels like she is today can fix it." She looks Frankie hard in the eyes. "Release us from the hex."

"But I *still* have no idea how to," Frankie says, throwing up her hands. "It's something else I don't remember."

Of course, even if she did, *should* she release them? Natas freaked her out with all that Oblivion stuff. The idea of a hex that could kill them does bother her, though. Would Mother *really* have cursed them like that?

"I'm not sure if I agree with what Mother did."

"You're not sure if you agree with yourself?"

"Hey, it's your fault, too," Frankie says, getting aggravated with Not-Estelle. "Why did you guys go inside the Oblivion in the first place? Didn't you know you might never come back out?"

Not-Estelle gets right up into Frankie's face, looking from one eye to the other, like it's some sort of examination. "You really *don't* remember very much, do you?"

"That's what I keep telling you."

Not-Estelle walks away, not answering Frankie's question. And her sister has another, more serious concern.

"Someone opened this soda already."

46

Sunday Supper

The zebra-striped wallpaper behind the booth is seriously aesthetic. Are they in some kind of old-fashioned nightclub? Were they celebrities? The woman sitting next to the Founder does look like a movie star.

Loud banging comes out of the kitchen, distracting Frankie from the black-and-white photo. Mr. Silvenus is purposefully making noise to show his irritation.

"He could at least be on time to dinner in his own apartment."

His apartment? Frankie scowls. *My apartment.*

This place feels like home the moment she walks in the door, in that way that home is a feeling. Maybe it's because the apartment is just how Mother left it. Except for these old photos, that is. They're nearly all of Dr. Natas from when he was Ramakrishna.

What a weird way to be vain.

The only photos not of the Founder are really, *really* old, like from Victorian times, and full of guys with big, bushy mustaches. Frankie squints at a portrait of two men. "Hey, is one of these him?" Frankie says, pointing.

"Yes," Mr. Silvenus says, poking his head out of the kitchen. "And the other is you."

Frankie is shocked.

"I was a man? With a *mustache*?" She leans in to look closer. "Which?"

"On the left."

"I'm not even the cute one."

She considers asking about what she—*he!*—was like, but the last thing Frankie needs is more confusion over her lives.

"Was Dr. Natas ever a woman?"

"Ask him yourself, if he ever shows up," Mr. Silvenus says. "This food is getting cold."

"Don't worry, he's coming," Frankie says.

Of everyone, Frankie can sense Dr. Natas's presence the strongest.

"He just walked inside the building."

"Finally!" Mr. Silvenus says. Frankie's locating powers still amaze her, but they don't phase her Latin teacher. He must be used to it after two thousand years. "I'll begin to 'plate,' as the people say."

Dr. Natas enters in the grumpiest mood ever.

"What a relief, to dine without the multitudes," he says when he sits down at the table.

"Speaking of multitudes, why do yet more spirits roam the grounds?" Mr. Silvenus says, looking down at Dr. Natas while he tosses the salad. "I haven't felt any seismic activity lately."

"Someone could be going inside the Oblivion and letting them out," Frankie says.

Dr. Natas looks up from his pasta, irritated by both of them.

"Those are not the only two possibilities," he says, taking a bite. "Perhaps the breach is breaking apart."

Freezing in the middle of serving the salad, Mr. Silvenus suddenly looks sick. "Why would you say that?"

"No breach lasts forever," Dr. Natas says.

"I wonder if that's why I didn't have any signal yesterday," Frankie says. "My phone didn't work when I was right under the cell tower. Then I met a spirit outside the gate."

"Oh dear," Mr. Silvenus says, sitting down.

"She wasn't like the others, either," Frankie says. "The woman didn't even seem to know she was dead, and only figured it out when she was talking to me."

"It can be rather confusing to die," Dr. Natas says, twirling spaghetti around his fork. "To separate on purpose is one thing; to be forcibly evicted from your body is quite another. Take it from me."

"But the thing is," Frankie says, "she remembered her life. She hadn't forgotten yet."

"A recent death, then," Dr. Natas says. "As I told you, the cleansing of memory takes time."

"And you and me?" Frankie says. "Why don't we forget?"

"That, my dear Frances, is a question for another evening," Dr. Natas says. He turns to Mr. Silvenus. "Would you please pass me the wine?"

Mr. Silvenus ignores the request, filling his own glass instead. "I do not like ghosts," he says, and takes a drink.

47

Weft into Warp

Carrying the spinning wheels down into the basement is way easier than bringing their replacements out of it, not because the looms are heavy but because they're so bulky. Even with a counselor on each corner it's awkward, and getting them through the art room door seems downright impossible no matter how much angling and tilting they do. Eventually, each loom somehow fits.

"Weaving marks the final step in the cloth-making process," Mr. Silvenus says once they begin, "as this marks the final week of our summer retreat."

The first-time weavers gather around Wilma giving a demonstration.

"The vertical threads strung across the shed of the loom are called the *warp*, while the unspooling thread is the *weft*," Mr. Silvenus explains. "The shuttle is the tool Wilma uses to weave weft into warp. From its constant journeying back and forth across the loom, we get our modern sense of the word, as *shuttles* convey passengers between two points."

Demo over, Frankie and the others take their seats. Unlike spinning, weaving comes back to her right away. As Mr. Silvenus wanders the room, lecturing, Frankie works the shuttle across the loom, back and forth, weft into warp, building a fabric one line of thread at a time.

"With the spinning wheel, we saw how the twisting of fibers into a thread came to symbolize the destiny of one person's life," Mr. Silvenus says. "A loom, on the other hand, crosses these threads, passing them through one another in a set pattern of intersections."

Back and forth, the shuttle across the loom, weft into warp.

"This retreat is the period during which *our* lives have intersected, and the fabric you weave will be the product of our crossed destinies."

It's hard to believe that the retreat is almost over. *Only four more days*. What's going to happen next? Is Frankie really going to go back to Flemington—for a month? That's what Lucie thinks she's doing, and probably Mom, too.

Frankie still doesn't know how to feel about Mom, and she's been avoiding even the thought of facing her. She can't bear it. She remembers her mother in Pompeii—Luna's mom—and imagines her as one of those plaster casts, forever locked in her moment of dying. The idea of her own mom dying makes Frankie want to cry again.

Back and forth, weft into warp.

The weaving is like a physical mantra, but it doesn't choke out her emotions. Because how can she not feel for her mom? *Crossed destinies*. If the lives of everyone in this room are woven together after just a month, how much more intertwined are she and Mom?

Part of Frankie wants to run away again. Sal and Jamie said she always has a place to stay. Or she can just get on a bus or train to it doesn't matter where—Missouri, Minnesota, or some other state that doesn't sound real.

But first, she has to finish this cloth.

Weft into warp.

48

The Ruins

The running of the shuttle across the loom worms its way so far into Frankie's brain that her mind keeps repeating the action during meditation. Even in bed, she dreams of warp and weft, her hand working the shuttle. It's a calm dream, until she realizes she's out of thread and thinks, *I'd still have some if I hadn't taken all those bus rides.* She needs to find more if she's ever going to finish, but she can't. The sheep are all shorn, and the grass is dead.

The anxiety builds and builds until it wakes Frankie up and she's thankful to realize it was just a dream.

But the anxiety doesn't go away.

Spirits are escaping. Frankie can feel it. And she can feel where it's happening.

The ruins.

For late July, the night is bizarrely cool, and Frankie pulls on a long-sleeve shirt to walk. Even before she gets near the lake, a shadow sweeps past her. She should've brought a jacket.

At the lake, the ice has spread to the middle—the part where she fell in. *Where I remembered.*

The jumble of fallen walls and rocks fills her with the most intense sense of foreboding yet. Frankie remembers walking this shoreline before, the last time she saw the Boathouse intact. Then, it led her to the sisters, suspended in midair, their bodies empty of their souls.

Who will she find this time? For a moment, she's convinced it will be Dr. Natas, but she can feel his body back home.

Light emanates from the fallen building, a glow like when she found the crystals down in the boiler room. Frankie finds the source in the collapsed facade, rising through the doorway that leads into the earth. She peers in. It's so deep. What's down there? A cellar? Another crypt? Or something else?

Because what if the breach *is* collapsing in on itself? What if, just below her feet, the Oblivion lies cracked open, a chasm she can fall into? The mere mention of the breach failing terrified Silvenus. Should she just leave?

A shadow shoots out of the abyss. Frankie loses her footing and almost falls in, but manages to tumble backward instead. She turns to see where the spirit went, and watches the ice spread farther. Frankie pulls the sleeves of her shirt down to cover her hands.

Mustering up her courage, Frankie sits and begins to levitate. Hovering, she moves herself over the open doorway and resists gravity like when she was the pearl. Descending, the glow grows brighter, revealing a cavernous underground chamber. Rusting tanks and a rotted wooden staircase lie toppled in a carpet of rubble.

Floating above the disorder is the source of the glow: two seated figures hovering just off the ground. Their skin is incandescent, their bodies radiating heat as well as light. Just like with the sisters.

For a moment, Frankie is convinced it's them, but of course it's not. They're trapped. Then Frankie thinks it must be Efrat and Ek. Why, she isn't sure. But it's not them, either.

It's Cadmus and Wilma.

The lips of the old man and her best friend are slightly parted.

Their breathing is loud, like the sound your throat makes when you fog up glass. Their eyelids are also parted, but only the whites of their eyes are visible, and this is the part of their bodies that glows most brightly of all.

What should Frankie do?

Before she can do anything, the shine in Wilma's eyeballs is extinguished, and the whites of them turn black. Then, like smoke, a shadow exits.

It exits *her eyes*.

The spirit makes an awful screech, fleeing through the fallen doorway above, and Wilma's eyes change again. They go white, but no longer glow; her pupils roll back into place. She stares at Frankie for a minute, in that way Wilma stares when she's sizing up everything about you. She closes her mouth, then opens it again.

"Grandfather," Wilma says. "We've been discovered."

─── INTERMEDIUS ───

The sound of the girl hurrying down the hall. He would know these footsteps no matter the where or the when. Her physical features change from one life to the next, but her footsteps, these remain constant.

Where could Frances be racing off to at this hour? None of the other children have stirred, so it's not for one of their late-night escapades. The old satyr puts down his book and goes to the window. From the brick walkway she turns right onto the main road, toward the front gate. Is she running away again?

The cold seeps through the glass panes, and Silvenus unfolds a blanket to drape over his legs as he returns to his wingback armchair. A wool blanket, at the end of July. *These spirits*, he thinks, sighing.

Could the gate truly be collapsing? Lord knows such things happen. Even here, once, when the Institute was still a sanatorium, and Frances was Cornelius. That was a confusing life for her; Silvenus is glad she didn't press him to know more when she saw the photograph.

Helene Margot is the life he longed to illuminate. She was a remarkable woman for those times. Or rather, for anyone in any time. Helene was all action, so different from Mother, who lived inside her studies. Frances is a combination of the two. At least, it pleases the satyr to think so.

Out in the hall, more noise. Rattling. *A spirit, inside of Croton!* The old man-goat huddles inside his woolly plaid cover, but it is only another of the students, visiting the bathroom. Silvenus sighs at his cowardice, and considers the other possible source of the phantom infestation.

The previous autumn, Silvenus believed Natas to be the culprit. What he failed to consider until Frances mentioned the possibility is that someone else could be responsible. That first time a spirit appeared and chased him through the woods, he now recalls, it occurred the day students began to arrive for fall semester with their parents. Or, in one case, their grandparent.

What if Cadmus entered the Oblivion that night?

An improbable notion. First, that he could enter without assistance, and second, that he would break his oath to Mother, particularly with her so close to waking.

Still, there always was something about the way Cadmus asked him to put Wilma and Frances in the same room together that bothered him. Natas told him not to, but Silvenus felt it was a trifling request to grant a dying man. Could it somehow be connected? Something so devious would seem patently beneath Cadmus. Yet, if history teaches us anything, it is that the moral compass of humans is not fixed, particularly when faced with their own impending demise.

PART THREE

THE DESCENT

49

Broken Promises

Frankie is FREAKING out. She just saw a spirit exit Wilma's *face*.

She can't believe it. It was *Cadmus* who let the spirits out last year. Cadmus and Wilma together! And they're doing it again!

Wilma is telling her to calm down.

"Calm down? *Calm down?* What about Rule One, Wilma? *Rule One!*"

"There's a good reason," Wilma says, but Frankie isn't listening. She's piecing everything together.

"You *knew* all year where the spirits were coming from, even when you said it was because of me!"

"I was kidding."

"Don't fang smile me, Wilma!"

"It's not her fault."

Frankie turns to Cadmus, back inside of himself.

"It was my idea to enter the Oblivion."

His saying the words out loud makes it even worse.

"How are you doing this? *Why* are you doing this?" Frankie says. "You're friends with the sisters! You see what happened to them."

"Mother, you know why I'm doing this." He speaks calmly, like he's talking down a hysterical person, which at the moment Frankie most certainly is.

"Don't 'Mother' me!" Frankie says. "And I don't have any *idea* why you're doing this!"

"For the same reason the sisters did. Because of what *you* told me," Cadmus says. "About how you got the gift."

"What are you talking about?"

"Going inside the Oblivion, when you were Luna," Cadmus says, floating closer to her. "That's how you got immortal memory."

Frankie steps away from him, tripping over some rubble.

He's saying this is her fault? That *she* got the gift from going inside the Oblivion? Dr. Natas said the sisters went there looking for immortality, but made it sound crazy. Did he mean immortal *memory*? Frankie is confused—and it's not the point.

"You can die, do you know that?" Frankie says. "You can go in and never come back out."

"A risk well worth taking," he says. "The joy of seeing you again convinced me, Mother."

"Stop *calling* me that."

"But you are her," Cadmus says. "I can see it. You're just like her."

"You being Mother—getting her memories back—you showed it's possible," Wilma says. "That someone other than Dr. Natas can get the gift."

Frankie feels ganged up on. Claustrophobic. She wants to get out of this dark underground pit.

"There will be no goodbye," Cadmus says, taking Frankie's hand. "That's what you told me before you died. You promised that I would see you again, and I have."

A vision comes to Frankie, of Mother's room in the apartment, of Cadmus seated at her bedside, his hand holding her own, like now. Having died so many times, she knew death was on its way.

"Grief is never being able to speak to your loved ones again," Cadmus says, "and the gift is the only remedy."

Wilma nods along.

"I haven't got much time left," he says, now shaking both of Frankie's hands, pleading. "I don't fear what's going to happen to my body. I'll be glad to shed it. I only want to hold on to the knowledge of my own experiences. Memory—*that* is the true soul."

It's like with Dr. Natas. You think one thing, then he turns you all around. *Listen last with your ears.* This is what Mother had to make sure she knew: Don't trust what someone is telling you when your mind and eyes tell you they're manipulating you. Frankie won't let Cadmus get away with it. Because:

"What about Wilma?" Frankie says. "She's got plenty of time left, but every time she goes in, she might never come out."

"You don't need to protect me," Wilma says.

"Except I do, because *he* certainly isn't protecting you." Frankie turns to Cadmus. "I *told* you it was dangerous. I *warned* you never to do it. And you swore to me you wouldn't."

Cadmus's face turns stony. "I thought you said you weren't Mother."

"No, I told you not to *call* me Mother," Frankie says, feeling more Mother than ever. "Like all the times I told you that the memory isn't a gift—it's a curse."

"That's for Grandpa to decide," Wilma says, frantic for Frankie not to ruin everything. "You have it already—you can't take it from him! Not when he's so close."

That's when it hits Frankie. Cadmus isn't the one she should be mad at.

"You've been using me," she says to Wilma. "You weren't kidding. I *am* the reason the spirits are here. You knew who I was before you even met me. That's why you told Lucie I'm

Mother—because you knew it would get me to come back."

"I didn't know anything, I—"

"The reason the spirits only get out when I'm here is because you two can only get into the Oblivion *when I'm here*. I'm just a power source to you."

"That is not true, Mother," Cadmus says.

"I won't let you go back in," Frankie says. "I'll leave, and you won't be able to separate."

"You can't do that!" Wilma says, panicked and angry. "You can't make that choice. That's not a friend!"

"No. No, she's right, Wilma," Cadmus says, trying to calm the situation. "I've been selfish. A selfish old man. And worse. Reckless. I should have never let you help me."

"Don't say that!" Wilma shouts at her grandfather.

Fueled as much by rage as her channeling abilities, Wilma bursts into the air up through the fallen doorway. Not like she's levitating, or how Cadmus steps on air, but true flying.

How did she do that?

50
Consequential

Random blades of straw and hay stick to her shoes, slick with morning dew. Crowding through the open gate, the sheep push past her, the ones shorn by Lonnie and Ox smooth, the ones clipped by the rest of them marked by random tufts of wool. It must have felt so good, to have all that thick, grimy wool sheared off. Like freedom. Frankie wishes she could feel that way.

Instead, she feels weighted down by the spirits that Cadmus and Wilma let out last night. They're everywhere. She can sense Cadmus and Wilma, too, inside their room.

Frankie helped Cadmus get back to the Mothership last night. He expended too much effort getting into the Oblivion to make it on his own. At least, that's what he said. What he really wanted was another chance to convince Frankie to help him.

"It's because her mother died so young that Wilma can't bear to also lose me forever," he said. Which might be true but was so manipulative.

This not working, Cadmus tried a different tack.

"If you come in with me, then Wilma won't have to."

Which was even more manipulative.

"Why do you need either of us to go in with you?" Frankie said as they crossed campus. "Once you separate, you can go inside alone."

Cadmus smiled. "But I might not remember to come out."

Pro tip: Always enter the Oblivion on the buddy system.

"What is it you have to do once you're inside, anyway?" Frankie said. "How can you tell when you get the gift?"

"If only you had told me that part," Cadmus said, smiling weakly. "All I know is that I have yet to travel as far as Luna did, and that I'm running out of time. In many ways."

Argus looks up at Frankie in the feed stall. Unfortunately for him, only the dregs at the bottom of the tub of kibble are left. She scrapes up what she can with the scoop and pours it into his bowl. The dog looks down, then back up at her. *Is this the best you can do?*

"Sorry, boy."

What Frankie is truly sorry for is that she's the reason for them wanting to enter the Oblivion. Why would Mother tell Cadmus how she got the gift? And the sisters!

Closing up the sheepfold, Frankie considers talking to Dr. Natas, but what if he does something to Cadmus? Or worse, to Wilma? The hex that Mother put on the sisters is one thing; what Dr. Natas does to Listeners who break the rules, she's pretty sure, is more than just the threat of death. *Fred.* The name pops into her head again, and she doesn't even want to think of why.

When Frankie and Cadmus arrived back at his room, there was no sign of Wilma.

"Don't worry, she'll be fine," Cadmus said as Frankie helped him to the bed. "And she won't stay mad at you."

Her stay mad at me? Frankie's the one who got betrayed. Her roommate is the only person Frankie completely confided in, and Wilma was deceiving her from the start.

Of course, no matter how furious she is at Wilma, it's not like she wants her to die.

"Promise me you won't go back in," Frankie said to Cadmus right before she left. "For real this time."

Cadmus looked up into her eyes.

"Is what I want so wrong?"

"The question isn't whether an action is right or wrong," Frankie said, the words popping into her head, "but the consequences."

Cadmus smiled, laying his head down on his pillow. "You and your sayings, Mother." He chuckled. "I promise."

He sounded like a little boy, like when she read to him.

Watching Argus eat his kibble, Frankie feels an ache inside of her that she hasn't ever felt before.

No, there's nothing so wrong with what you want.

51

Nighttime Drivers

Faster and faster, Wilma violently bangs the shuttle from one side of the loom to the other. It's unnerving everyone, and yet Frankie finds herself trying to go faster, not even wanting to, she just can't help being competitive. She's pretty sure that's true in every life, too.

"Weaving is not a race, girls," Mr. Silvenus says.

Banging the shuttle hard one last time, Wilma gets up and leaves. *Good,* Frankie thinks to herself, even though her heart really isn't in being mad. She yawns.

Five minutes later, Frankie falls asleep at her loom, and again behind the veil. Napping while levitating is surprisingly pleasant; Dr. Natas's tale of his life as a camel trader in the Gobi desert is the perfect bedtime story.

As the counselors get dinner ready, Ek is talking about how excited he is to move to Tokyo, when the wall phone rings in the vestibule.

"I'll get it," Ek says, leaving the kitchen.

"What was that with you and Wilma on the looms this morning?" Lucie says, pulling a tray of food out of the fridge.

Before Frankie can say *Nothing*, Ek yells, "Hey, Lucie! Phone call for you!"

"Oh, wow, that's awesome!" Frankie hears her brother say. "Okay, cool! We'll see you soon, Mom."

Frankie is annoyed that Mom only asked for Lucie. Relieved, also.

"Great news!" Lucie says, coming back into the kitchen. "Mom got the day off from work Friday so she can come pick us up with the rest of the parents."

How is that great news? Frankie still has no idea what to say to her. Should she just pretend like nothing is different?

On the other hand, maybe she should see if Mom can come right now, since Frankie leaving is the only way to be sure Cadmus and Wilma can't go back into the Oblivion. As it is, it's going to take days to capture all the spirits they let out last night.

She gets mad at Cadmus and Wilma all over again, and the whole time they're out trapping shadows that evening. Thank god Lonnie and Diana are there.

"We've done this before," Lonnie says, having just caught a spirit haunting the study hall. "The summer of '78—now *that* was an infestation."

The final shade Frankie locates that night leads them to the garages. At the side door, Frankie gets the key from under the moss-covered mat and tells the rest of the spirit hunters to wait outside while she goes in. Parked on the other side of the golf cart is the Founder's Jaguar. The driver's seat is occupied.

Shadow hands grip the steering wheel as the ghost woman desperately tries to remember how she got here. *It had something to do with driving,* she thinks. Her face is nearly as blank as her mind, showing only a flickering hint of her features.

"You don't need this?" Moira says, holding up a bottle as Frankie locks the garage.

"False alarm," Frankie says, putting the key back under the mat.

"Are you sure there's no spirit in there?" Ox says. "It's so bloody cold..."

∽

In her room past midnight, Frankie is keeping mental tabs on Cadmus and Wilma, who, thankfully, remain in the Mothership. Frankie nods off at some point and wakes up in the morning, late. Her first thought: *Did they go in again?*

She doesn't feel any new spirits. But she also hasn't had coffee yet. Caffeine definitely helps with the whole detecting spirits thing.

Down at breakfast, everyone's already eating.

"Can you believe what happened last night?" Lucie asks her.

Oh no.

"What is it?"

"The golf cart."

"The *golf* cart?"

52

The Golf Cart Incident

No one can get over how wrecked it is. The passenger side is practically sheared off, with both wheels flat and at busted angles.

After it hit whatever caused the damage, the cart must've flipped, because its roof is half crushed.

"What happened?" Frankie says.

"Dunno, mate," Ox says. "Must've been spirits."

"Why would a spirit do this to a golf cart?" Lucie says.

"Maybe it was the ghost of Tiger Woods."

"Tiger Woods is still alive, Moira," Ek says.

Having secured one end of a chain to the cart's front axle, Bob hooks the other to the rear hitch of the tractor.

Frankie can tell there are no new shadows this morning (*thank you, coffee*), which leaves exactly one spirit that could have done this. She kicks herself; Frankie should've sent that ghost woman into a bottle last night when she had the chance.

"I loved that golf cart," Lucie says, watching Bob tow it away.

On the plus side, Cadmus kept to his promise. For one night, anyway.

That afternoon, Dr. Natas makes a surprise visit while the kids finish cleaning up lunch.

"Will all of my counselors please come and have a seat," Dr. Natas says.

He, however, remains standing.

"Do any of you have some*thing* to tell me?"

"About what?" Ek says.

"What do you think?" Dr. Natas says.

"The golf cart?" Lucie says.

Before Dr. Natas can respond, Moira bursts into tears.

Like, sobbing.

She'd make a really bad spy.

"We didn't mean to wreck it . . . ," Moira says between heaving breaths. "We . . . we just wanted to . . ."

"We?" Efrat says.

Everyone turns to look at Ox.

"All right, mates. You got me," the oversize deem says. "Yeah, I wrecked the thing. It was dark and we were going down the hill and I didn't see the rock."

Moira is sniffling.

Dr. Natas holds his arm toward the exit. "Mr. Oxnard," he says, "after you."

"How about *her*?" Ox says with a WTF look.

Moira bursts into sobs again.

Dr. Natas stares at him like he's drilling a hole into Ox's skull with his eyes.

"Whatever," Ox says, getting up and walking past Dr. Natas out the door.

༺༻

"They've been in his office a long time," Lucie says.

So long that the Listeners are twenty minutes late going behind the veil. They're huddled in a corner of Chapel talking, Cadmus among them. Not staying up half the night in the Oblivion must give him extra energy.

"Do you think Ox is going to get fired?" Lucie says to the other counselors.

"That's hardly a punishment," Efrat says. "The retreat is over in three days. He should get suspended from school. Or expelled."

"How long does it take to fire *or* expel someone?" Lucie says.

Ek is shaking his head. "It's not the Pythagorean Institute way," he says, "to cast people aside for a mistake."

Moira isn't there. She ran to her room after Dr. Natas took Ox and hasn't come out since.

Frankie remembers her own trips to the principal's office. Has Dr. Natas broken out the tea? Is Ox drinking it?

Crossing Chapel to where the counselors are sitting is Diana. She stops in front of Frankie. "We've been chatting," she says, "and we think *you* should run today's session."

The other kids stare at her. Frankie's been going behind the veil for all of a week and they're asking *her* to lead it? The other counselors might never guess that she's Mother, but they still know something's off. What should she tell them?

"Just go," Efrat says.

Walking away with Frankie, Diana whispers with a wink, *"Just like you used to lead us!"* Of course, she says it way too loudly.

Down in the crypt, Frankie feels awkward as Lonnie lights the fire in the altar and the others assemble themselves in a circle. Wilma's hostile presence doesn't help, either. The Listeners snap, waiting on Frankie to begin—to tell them a story of one of her past lives.

She swallows hard as the snapping dies down. *I've got nothing.* If only she had her moleskin journal with her. Frankie thinks about telling a story from *this* life but is so flustered she can't think of one. Even the skulls are staring at her, waiting. She'd never seen a human skull before coming down here, but is it really different from any other animal's?

"I was a hawk," Frankie begins, looking to Diana, then Eeva. She holds out her palms. "Spreading your wings—it feels the same as spreading your fingers. You don't feel the feathers any more than you feel the skin on your arms or the hair on your head, because they're just you. But the air—catching you, holding you—the air you feel as solidly as the ground beneath your feet."

Eyes now closed, Frankie holds out her arms as wide as they can go. It must look ridiculous, but she doesn't care. She's flying.

"Beating your wings against the wind is like running up a mountain—slow and difficult. Turning the other way, however, the gusts at your tail, nothing can go faster than you."

Scattered snapping starts again, now louder.

"The best breezes are those where the land meets the sea. You ride them, wings outstretched, allowing the air to hold you aloft. You drift."

Frankie releases her arms to her sides.

"Suddenly, there's a squall. The rain is ferocious; the thunder, disorienting. Violent gusts sweep you away, make you dizzy. When at last the storm fades, you attempt to get your bearings, but there is only endless sea, and with the air now still, you must keep beating your wings; to rest is to die. But they're aching, exhausted. Your heart pumps faster, from the effort, from the terror. You must land, but there is no land to land, only water, and *I can't swim*."

Frankie's eyes open. The snapping has risen to a roar of approval.

"I don't know why I told that story," she says.

"Because all of us feel lost and helpless," Agent Y says. "Sometimes."

By the time the Listeners get out, Ox is also out.

Not fired, not expelled.

"That's not the Pythagorean Institute way," Ek repeats, happy to have his beliefs confirmed.

But *is* it Ox? He acts like an entirely different person, staying until the end of dinner cleanup and then asking for something more to do.

"There *is* nothing more to do," Efrat says. "Go play foosball or whatever."

Instead, Ox goes back to his room without even pausing to make fun of the way Efrat says *foose*-ball.

"Does Dr. Natas have the power to control minds, too?" Efrat says.

53

Playground

The good Ox isn't a one-night-only event. For two full days, he's been acting helpful, even kind.

It's the weirdest thing yet.

Dr. Natas may not have the power to control minds, but he sure can turn a person upside down. *He must've been like that when he was the Founder, too,* Frankie thinks as she passes his portrait.

She no longer even half bows to the paintings when she comes in, knowing who they are. *Who we are.* Still, it's hard for Frankie to see herself in Mother, even with the not-smiling smile. What the Founder shares with Dr. Natas is obvious: the eyes. Not the eyes themselves, but the shape around them—the squint, the position of the eyebrows. How did she never notice before?

Upstairs in his apartment, Frankie asks Dr. Natas why he didn't bring Moira into his office the other day.

"There is nothing I can tell the girl about her actions that she does not already know," he says. "Mr. Oxnard, on the other hand, has quite a bit to learn. Mistakes are teaching opportunities, as you always said."

Frankie is tired of everyone quoting Mother back to her.

"How did leading the Listeners go? Flawlessly, I hear," Dr. Natas says, answering his own question. "Your memory appears to be improving."

Penny told Frankie she got goose bumps from the hawk story. "It was exactly like when you were Mother," she said. "The Founder always gives us a little biography of his past lives. You share the *experience* of living them."

But Frankie didn't come here to talk about the Listeners, and certainly not about Ox or Moira.

"I know how I got the gift," she says.

Dr. Natas gives her a look like she's finally said something interesting.

"Really?" he says. "Tell me, how *did* you get it?"

"By breaking Rule One," Frankie says. "When I was Luna."

"Luna certainly was not one for following rules," Dr. Natas says. "You never are."

"But I don't remember how I made it inside the Oblivion," Frankie says. "How I managed to separate."

"Separating is like channeling," Dr. Natas says. "The level

of what you can achieve depends not only on your proximity to a breach, but the strength of that breach. And the breach in Pompeii, well..."

Dr. Natas shakes his head.

"Was it as strong as the one here?" Frankie says.

"No," he says with a *perish-the-thought* look. "It was exponentially stronger. The intensity of a rift correlates to the seismic energy that created it, and the earthquake that destroyed Pompeii was massive in the extreme."

"But a volcano destroyed Pompeii."

"That was the rebuilt city. Seventeen years before Vesuvius exploded, an earthquake devastated the seaward-facing slope of the mountain. The intervening period was the most ex*traordinary* time to channel." Dr. Natas makes a face like he's remembering the greatest meal of his life. "The breach was so significant that even a child could exit their body. An exceptional child, I grant you, but a child nevertheless."

Frankie does love a compliment, even if it's for a former life. Still, it doesn't answer the question she came to ask.

"How did going inside help me remember my past lives?"

"The Oblivion was your playground. Luna's playground." Dr. Natas leans forward, telling the story like he would behind the veil. "Luna told the Listeners that she never got lost inside, and that she always came out before she began to forget too much." Before Frankie can ask, he says, "Oh yes, there were Listeners then, too. Hundreds. They followed me from Rome to Pompeii. And you—Luna—became one of them, because you proved what you could do. You entered the Oblivion for an entire day and returned to tell the tale." He smiles, remembering. "In recent lives, you've come up with the theory that Luna's many trips caused her to build up a re*sistance* to the Oblivion."

"Resistance? Like to a cold?"

"Call it an inoculation. A vaccine against the permanent erasure of memory." Dr. Natas gives Frankie a skeptical look. "Again, this is *your* theory. I have never been convinced."

"Why not?"

"Because it never worked for anyone else." He shrugs. "Of course, those who try rarely come back alive, unless they are dragged back. Hence, Rule One."

Frankie is all the more relieved that Cadmus and Wilma haven't tried going inside again. It's been three days now.

"So if building up a resistance isn't what gave me the gift, what did?"

Dr. Natas shrugs again.

"Perhaps you were born with it," he says. "Maybe the gift is what allowed you to slip so easily inside the Oblivion in the first place. Even with the magnitude of the Pompeiian breach, you remained the only one of the Listeners able to separate by yourself. A fact that has held true in every one of your lives."

"Are you saying I'll be able to do that, too?"

"Oh, Frances, I am quite certain that you already *can*," Dr. Natas says.

As Frankie gets up to leave, she realizes something.

"Your earthquake relief organization—that's about finding new breaches in the Oblivion, isn't it? More powerful ones. And a backup, in case the one here really does collapse." Now it's Frankie giving the skeptical look. "Is all of your help-save-the-world stuff fake?"

Dr. Natas raises an eyebrow, smiling.

"You have had a most suc*cessful* retreat, Frances," he says. "I do hope you enjoy the final day tomorrow."

54
All Good Things

Friday is sad for everyone, filled with last-day-ism. *Our last day weaving! Our last day behind the veil!*

For Frankie, it's less sad than excruciating, because of what's coming at the end of the day. Because of *who* is.

"I can't wait to see your mother," Diana says at lunch. "It's been years."

Somehow, the thought hadn't occurred to Frankie that the Listeners knew Mom. But of course they do.

"Lucie reminds me so much of her."

After making sure no one can overhear, Frankie asks, "When my mom adopted me, did you guys know who I was?"

"No," Diana says, grinning. "But we had our *suspicions*."

Ox offers to stay after lunch and clean up alone so the others can go back to the loom to finish their textiles.

"Really, I don't mind."

"You're starting to freak me out, Ox," Frankie says. She's happy to have the extra time, though. In the art room, Frankie works the shuttle, continuing even after the others have left. At a few minutes to four, she picks up a pair of scissors, cuts the threads across the warp, and ties the ends off like Mr. Silvenus showed them. Pulling the finished product off the loom, she holds it up, proud. *Wilma has to see this*, Frankie thinks, then remembers they're mad at each other. Wilma hasn't left her room today, so there's not much chance she'll get to show it to her.

She rolls up the fabric and writes her name on the back.

Frankie C.

That done, she runs all the way to Chapel just to have Dr. Natas tell her she isn't going behind the veil.

"Your mother is here," he says. "Go see her. I promise, you will not miss anything you have not heard before."

"But it's the final day of the retreat," Frankie says. "Can't Lucie go?"

"She wants to see you alone, Frances."

55

Babysitting

Outside the window, the farm stand passes by, stacked with pints of berries and tomatoes. Normally, she'd ask her mother if they could stop and get some, but she feels too uneasy to ask anything, even where they're driving to. Frankie has never felt this way around her mom. Angry with her, lots of times, but not like she's sitting with a stranger.

At least she finally gets to be in the front.

You think it's hot up HERE?

"That's a good one," Mom says. "I always liked the signs."

"Were they here when you worked at the school?" Frankie says, turning to her.

Mom nods. Frankie nods, too.

"When did you find out that I know who I am?" Frankie asks.

"Dr. Natas called me after you got back from California," Mom says, her eyes on the road. "It was part of our deal, that he'd tell me. I didn't want to bother you. It must be . . . quite something. To deal with."

Mom says this all in the most un-Mom way possible. Timidly. Frankie asks, "Mom, are you afraid of me?"

"You *were* my boss," Mom says with a nervous laugh.

"I *am* your daughter," Frankie says. "And I was never your boss. I'm not Mother. I just, like, have some of her memories."

"Don't lie to make me feel better, Frances."

"When have I ever done that?" Frankie says.

Mom grips the steering wheel tighter. "But you *are* her," she says, a more familiar edge creeping into her voice. "You weren't even five the first time I saw it."

"When I was in pre-K you saw that I was a seventy-year-old psychiatrist from Shanghai?"

"It was *that*."

"It was what?"

"The sarcasm. No child was ever so sarcastic at so young an age."

"So is that why you always treated me like you did? Not because I was adopted but because I reminded you of Mother?"

"Reminded?" Mom says. "The way you stand, the way you hold a fork, that withering look you're giving me right now—it doesn't remind me of Mother, it *is* Mother."

Mom pulls over to the side of the road and shuts the car off. She always does this right before she yells at Frankie.

"Don't you get it?" Mom says, her anger rising. "I wasn't asked to be your mother, I was asked to be your *babysitter*. Not until your parents got home from dinner—until you woke up. And when you woke up, you'd realize that you were this brilliant woman who wrote books and started schools and lived dozens of incredible lives. And then you'd remember who I was—some dumb girl from nowhere New Jersey you hired as a favor to her older brother."

Frankie can't believe this. Isn't *she* the one who's supposed to be upset?

"Are you seriously trying to make me feel bad right now?" Frankie says. "After you spent my whole life lying to me and making me feel like you loved Lucie more than me? Which you do!"

"So it's all about you, is it, Frances?"

"It's *never* been about me."

"That's where you're wrong." Mom sticks a finger in her face. "It's **always** been about you."

Frankie folds her arms and goes back to staring out the window. They're in an unpopulated stretch of woods, and the car shakes as a truck speeds by. Mom adjusts her rearview mirror, just to do something. Then she sighs.

"Frances, I'm sorry if I could be mean to you," Mom says, letting go of her defensiveness. "I resented you, it's true, and I know that's not fair. The reason is that I always knew that this day would come. This awful day."

She hides her face in her hands.

"But don't you love me, Mom?" Frankie says.

"Of course I love you!" Mom says, her voice breaking. "I just never felt like I was *supposed* to."

Frankie leans across the armrest with the old soda cups to hug her.

"Of course you're supposed to. You're my mom!" Frankie says. "And I love *you*."

"You don't have to," Mom says, crying. "I don't want you to feel guilty—to be nice to me because you feel bad."

"Again—when I have I *ever* done that?" Frankie says.

Mom does that cry-laugh thing, and blows her nose in an old fast-food napkin.

God, this car is a mess.

⁕

They sit there for a while in the Prius, talking. Not about Mother or Dr. Natas or being in a cult, but about everything else.

Frankie never realized that Mom also grew up in the shadow of a brother. Uncle Sal was always better at school and he never got into trouble like she did. "And your grandmother always loved him best."

Obviously, her past lives aren't the only cycles being repeated. The crazy thing is how her mom doesn't even notice.

"You're going to have to tell Lucie that you used to work at the school," Frankie says.

"I know," Mom says. She's clearly not looking forward to it. "Did you tell him you're adopted?" Frankie shakes her head no. "Do you want me to tell him?" Frankie again shakes no.

Mom said that Dr. Natas found Frankie when she was a year

old and that she was already an orphan. She never got the exact details because she didn't want to know.

"Why did you adopt me?" Frankie asks.

"Because Dr. Natas asked me to."

"That's it?" Frankie says. "He just asked?"

"He said you were the only person in the world who mattered to him. For Dr. Natas, this person who was like a god, to need *my* help? To trust *me* with you? How could I say no?" Mom shakes her head. "I was never good at anything else here. Definitely not channeling."

"Neither is Lucie."

"It must not run in the family," Mom says.

"But *I'm* good," Frankie says.

"I bet you are." Mom turns the car back on. "I bet you are," she repeats.

56

Toasted

At dinner, Mom is the guest of honor. The old hippies give her huge kisses and Dr. Natas delivers a toast, but it's Cadmus who's the chummiest, leaning over and talking into her ear. Frankie can't hear what he's saying, but Mom keeps laughing and Cadmus keeps topping off her wineglass.

Most everyone else is already gone. Efrat left in the morning and Ox's dad came a couple hours ago, picking up not just his son but Ek and Moira, both of whom have international flights out of New York in the morning. The Mysterions left at the same time, and Eeva just before dinner, having handed each of the counselors a thank-you card. She really is a politician.

With their plane scheduled to leave tomorrow afternoon, Wilma and Cadmus are the only ones supposed to stay the night, but the Caridis clearly won't be going anywhere, either.

"Being here was the happiest time of my life!" Mom says loudly. She is *so* drunk.

When Dr. Natas tells her that she can stay in the guest room of his apartment, Mom starts to cry again, she's so moved by the gesture. Frankie can't believe how she's falling over herself for him. Neither can Lucie.

Besides that she worked here, Frankie doesn't know exactly what Mom told Lucie, but he's been quiet all night. She asks if he's okay and her brother says he's fine, although he seems anything other than fine. When the siblings help Lonnie, Diana, and Penny carry their luggage to their Uber, Lucie still barely says a word, even when the old hippies are hugging him goodbye.

"You not being polite," Frankie says as they stand waving. "Now I know I need to be concerned."

"What do you want me to say?" Lucie says. "That you were right about Mom? That she never tells us the truth? That I worked for Dr. Natas all year and he never told me the truth, either?"

Actually, Frankie doesn't want to hear that at all. What she wants is for Lucie to know that it's okay to be upset—to get mad at people. "It just gives you the opportunity to forgive them," she says. Like she's being ironic, except she's not. She puts her arms around her little brother.

At first, Lucie is stiff; then he softens; then he squeezes her tightly.

"I'm gonna head to my room," he says when he finally lets go.

An hour later, Frankie isn't worried about her brother, she's worried about their mom falling down the steep staircase. She's tipsy, verging on wasted.

"Grab the rail, Mom."

She does, then turns back to stare Frankie in the eyes. She squints like she's trying to focus. "You never liked me very much, did you?"

"Come on, Mom, didn't we do this?" Frankie says, just wanting to get up to the apartment to put her to bed. "I love you."

"Not *you*, Frances," she says. "*You*, Mother."

Frankie sighs. "Mother liked you."

The truth is, however, she didn't. But that person isn't Frankie.

"You and Cadmus sure seem to be pals," Frankie says.

"Everyone loves Cadmus," Mom says. "Well, almost everyone."

"Who doesn't?"

"Him!" Mom says, pointing up the narrow stairwell to Dr. Natas's door. "He was always so jealous."

"Of what?"

Mom starts laughing. "You don't know?"

"No."

Drunk parents are the worst.

"**You**." Mom laughs again. "Cadmus was your favorite little foster son."

The laughing keeps echoing down the stairwell. Frankie really wishes Mom would stop.

57

Resuming Conversations

The full moon shines like a pale sun, making the campus brighter and less spooky than it should be with everyone gone.

Walking away from the Mothership slowly, Frankie regrets not having stopped by Wilma's room to talk. To tell her she's not mad at her anymore. Sure, it sucked that Wilma lied to her all year—*that's* not a friend—but what Wilma wants for her grandpa, well, who wouldn't want a loved one coming back to life?

As she thinks about turning back, the branches rustle above Frankie's head. It can't be from the wind; there is none.

"Join me!" Cadmus calls from up in the treetops. "Come on, it's easy!"

He gives Frankie a boost like she's never had before, sucking her off the ground. She scrambles to get her footing and finds it on the light twiggy branches like squirrels run on. They're springy, and Frankie hops from one to the next. She feels like a four-year-old in a bouncy castle, and what's better than that?

At the top, Cadmus offers a hand, and together they leap across the leaves of a maple tree like rocks in a stream. Cadmus looks at her, eyes smiling, reflecting the moon. Frankie remembers why she loved him so much. Why Mother did. Then he says, "One last walk among the trees!" and her heart sinks. She never likes a last, and this is a whole other level of last.

"Oh, don't be sad. This is joy!" Cadmus says, floating down to a low dogwood. "Do you remember the day you taught me how to do this? It was the summer of 1959. Or maybe it was '60." Before Frankie can *yeah-I-kinda-vaguely-do* pretend, he says, "No, I don't suppose you would."

"Why aren't you up here with Wilma?"

"I wanted to be alone tonight."

"Oh," Frankie says. "I can go."

"No, stay!" Cadmus says emphatically. "This way."

Using a pine tree as a ladder, they scale drooping branches up to a broad-leaved sycamore, the tallest tree on campus. The view from the top isn't much at night, but in her mind she sees the river winding through the valley.

"I always loved coming up here," Frankie says.

For once, Cadmus isn't looking to reminisce. His face turns serious.

"I want you to put all the spirits we let out back into the Oblivion. They should be preparing for their new bodies, not trapped inside of bottles."

Put spirits back into the Oblivion? Frankie sighs. "That's one more thing I don't remember how to do."

"Don't worry, you'll figure it out," he says. "I also very much want you and Wilma to stay friends."

"That's not only up to me."

"Wilma isn't mad at you," Cadmus says. "And you certainly can't be mad at her."

"Why not?" Frankie says.

Cadmus tilts his head. "You spend every one of your lives hiding your most important truths from those you love. How can you hold it against anyone else for doing the same thing?"

Fair point.

They don't speak for a minute.

"I'm sorry I can't help you," Frankie says. "I'm not sure you'd get what you want anyway."

"That's what *he* always said."

Meaning Dr. Natas. Frankie gets the distinct feeling that Cadmus doesn't like him much, either.

They go quiet again, and this time Cadmus breaks the silence. "You know, I was almost fifty when I found out that it wasn't all a lie."

"What wasn't?"

"Reincarnation," Cadmus says. "You had told me about it, of course, and the things I saw here—the things I could do here—proved that anything was possible. But *that*? Being reincarnated? Remembering past lives? Part of me was sure it had to be a hoax, that the two of you were frauds." Cadmus looks up at the moon. "It was ten years after the fire that you called me to come back. You didn't say why. When I pulled into the garages, this skinny boy from the Philippines was there waiting for me. He shook my hand and launched right into the middle of a conversation. I couldn't understand what was going on, until I realized that it was the same conversation I had with the Founder the last time I saw him. About the passenger pigeon, of all things." Cadmus turns away from the sky to face Frankie. His eyes, now entirely gray, stare into hers, from one to the other. "The experience is so very different with you."

Instead of walking back down the foliage, they float to the ground through the open air, resisting the fall, two pearls in the night. At the bottom, they go in separate directions.

"Goodbye, Frankie," Cadmus says.

58

On Thick Ice

When she wakes up, it's to the shakes and to sheets soaked in cold sweat. The temperature must have gone down thirty degrees from when she went to bed.

Frankie doesn't need coffee to tell that there are new spirits, or to know that the door to the Oblivion has been left open. Walking across the lake doesn't require channeling, either, as she arrives to find it completely covered in a thick sheet of ice.

Even before descending into the underground of the ruins, Frankie knows what she'll find. The two of them, seated as before, eyelids split open, spirits escaping.

"Wilma! Come on, Wilma! Come back to me!"

Should she shake her? Or would that be bad?

Screw it. She shakes her. Hard.

"Wilma! Come on!"

No luck. Cadmus is too fragile to shake so she just calls his name, over and over, but she can't bring him back either.

What do I do?

Frankie thinks about trying to separate. Dr. Natas said she could do it. But what about the buddy system? What if she gets lost and stays in the Oblivion too long and dies?

She has to talk to *somebody* before going inside, and it sure isn't going to be Dr. Natas.

That leaves one option.

To have Frankie come begging for help is sweet victory for Not-Estelle.

"Why should *we* help you do to someone else what you did to us?" she says. "When you don't even bring chips!"

"Chips? It's midnight! What chips?" Frankie says. "And I saved your lives."

"Who asked you to? We were on the brink of getting the gift—I'm sure of it," Not-Estelle says. "I hope Cadmus does get it. Why should only you and Natas have immortal memory? It's disgusting!"

"But what if he and the poor girl never come back out?" Estelle says. "He never told us he was bringing little Wilma into this."

"You guys knew this was going on?" Frankie says.

"Cadmus told us the day he arrived," Not-Estelle says proudly.

"What can we even say to help?" Estelle says. "You've forgotten more about channeling than we'll ever know."

"That's the problem," Frankie says. "I've forgotten almost everything!"

Not-Estelle looks at her harshly.

"This lack of self-confidence," she says. "You really aren't like her."

"*Now* you believe me?" Frankie says. "Look, I need to know how I found you guys inside—how I can find *them*."

"We can't give you directions like *turn left at the second stoplight* inside the Oblivion," Not-Estelle says. "The only way we can help is if we go in with you."

"But I still have no idea how to get rid of the hex, and Dr. Natas sure won't do it."

"Then you're on your own," Not-Estelle says.

"We'll see you when you get back!" Estelle says, waving goodbye like Frankie is going on vacation.

"*If* she gets back," her sister corrects her.

59

Orpheus

The body scan isn't working. Maybe it's the two glowing, soulless bodies with their eyes turned up into their skulls that's making her anxieties multiply, or maybe it's her fear of what will happen to her if she goes inside the Oblivion—or what will happen to these empty bodies if she doesn't.

Closing her eyes again, Frankie takes a long, deep inhale and goes to her most comforting place.

Omnia mutantur nihil interit

Repeating her mantra over and over, Frankie's mind drifts away from her anxieties, and then from the mantra itself. Ovid's poetry begins to flow, eventually wandering to a different tale altogether.

Orphea nequiquam voce vocatur

"He is called by the voice belonging to Orpheus," she translates to herself. Or maybe Mother does; Frankie got a B-minus on her Orpheus quiz.

He dared descend down to the Styx
Through the gate of Tenaerus.
Among the unreal throng,
Among the honored phantoms,
He reached the presence of Persephone and
Him who rules the murky realms:
The lord of shadows.

Pluto. That's who Orpheus came to the Underworld to see, to ask a favor—a big one. His wife Eurydice had died from a poison snakebite, and Orpheus wanted the lord of shadows to let her return to the world of the living.

Frankie wishes she could just stroll down to the Underworld like Orpheus, because how is she going to separate all on her own? She remembers being Luna and hardly even needing to try, that it was no more work than falling asleep. Her soul was—is—right there, hardly connected to anything. All it needs is the slightest permission to release. To be *allowed* to.

Suddenly, Frankie sees her body moving away from her. But her body isn't what's moving—her spirit is. She didn't even realize that she's already outside of herself.

Light now surrounds her, the same light that's radiating from the hovering bodies of Cadmus and Wilma. That glow *is* the Oblivion, seeping out of them, the same as it was with the crystals. All she has to do is give herself over to the light, and she'll be inside.

She hesitates.

Orpheus got what he came to the Underworld for. He managed to convince Pluto to reverse Eurydice's death and let her leave with him—on one condition: Never look back.

In a serious hurry to return to the world of the living, Orpheus got ahead of Eurydice on the path up. Forgetting the deal he made, Orpheus glanced behind his shoulder to make sure she was still there. The instant he did, Eurydice slipped away.

Reaching out, to hold and be held,
Nothing was held, alas, but fleeting air.

They both were doomed: Eurydice to stay in the Underworld, Orpheus to live in the world above, mourning his beloved wife for the rest of his days.

Let's hope this trip goes better for me.

Frankie enters the Oblivion.

60

Katabasis

She stands on the shore of the blue-black sea. Ships with sails like the wings of gulls cut through swelling waves. *That smell!* It's the smell of home.

Why did she ever leave? Where did she even go? And how did she come back?

Luna bends down to pick up a stone. Her thumb rubs its surface, smoothed by the sea, and its weight in her palm is satisfyingly heavy.

It's real.

So why are her arms coated in ash?

Like she always does when she's lost, the girl looks back for the peak of Vesuvius to orient herself, but it's gone. Right. Her city is gone; Pompeii is gone.

I am gone.

When the world was dying all around her, Luna fled to the Oblivion. That's where she is. *Don't let yourself forget who you are!*

But who is she? Not Luna.

She's Frankie. *I came inside to get Wilma.* So why does she feel like Luna? If only she had a mirror, to check.

Oh, wait. I do have a mirror. Because the sea is now a glassy lake.

Whoever she is, she gets on her hands and knees and looks down into the still surface of the water, peering carefully over the edge so as not to fall in. Staring back at her is a face she hasn't seen in two thousand years.

I was so pretty when I was Luna.

The day of the explosion, the noise was so loud. Deafening. In here is peace.

How is it this peaceful?

She wants to indulge in her reflection like Narcissus, to keep staring and never let go. Then she notices that her cheeks and forehead are covered with ash, too. She cups some water and splashes her face, then plunges her arms deep into the dark lake. After washing up to her shoulders, she lowers her mouth to take a sip.

Should I really be drinking the water?

Frankie stands to find that the lake is on the edge of a forest— the woods of the Institute.

Am I back inside the walls?

"Who is to say you ever left?"

Frankie turns to see a man. He's middle-aged, balding, and thin; he wears a toga. He looks nothing like himself, but the raised eyebrow, the smirk, his posture—it is exactly him. The dread and love she feels toward the man is the same, too.

When he inhabited this body, he led the Listeners of Rome and Pompeii, and called himself Valerius. That's not what Luna called him, however.

"Where is your father?" Silvenus kept asking over and over as the people fled for cover, shaking her, trying to save them both.

"You're my father," Frankie says to Natas.

He sighs. "Do not make this into a big deal, Frances."

"Why don't you call me Luna?"

"You know the rules," he says. "Only the most recent name. Things become confusing otherwise."

"But this first life—it was different."

"For you, certainly. For me, hardly." He walks closer to her. "Physical bodies are nothing more than temporary houses for the soul. No reason to get sentimental about them; there is always another body to move into, another set of parents."

"Are you kidding?" Frankie says. "Our parents don't just hatch us."

"Frances, we go through this every time. You have had sixty-six sets of parents that you re*call*—or someday will—and countless more before them. So I happened to be your biological father, once. What does it matter?"

"Maybe I inherited the gift from you," she says. "Wouldn't it matter then?"

He shakes his head no.

"Of all my children, you are the only one," he says. "You attained the power some other way."

"I followed you inside the first time, didn't I? I saw what you were doing."

"Who knows how and when children discover the secrets of their parents?" he says. "When I found out what you were doing, I forbid you to enter. But you were a willful child. Always challenging me. And your mother. Oh, did you make life hard on your mother."

The vision of her mother comes to her. Those long, tight curls that spilled across her forehead. Tears come to her eyes. God, if she could only see her again.

"Come, let us stroll together."

61

The Journey Not the Destination

They walk through the forest together, barefoot. Valerius has his hands clasped behind his back, like the men who stroll down the decumanus maximus, their togas pulled tight over their bellies. And now that's where they are, in the crowded main street of Pompeii. All these men—these ladies and children—she knows them.

Luna's thoughts come pulsing back. She looks through the crowd for Marcellus, the boy she had a crush on. She sees his face in her mind perfectly.

He was seriously hot.

But he died, two thousand years ago. What a waste. Buried under the ash, like her mother, her sisters, her father. And herself, too.

She thinks of the man lying on his back, arms up, trying to block the falling pumice rocks from hitting him.

"Did anyone survive?"

"Silvenus. He hired a boat." Father smiles. "That satyr has an unerring sense of self-preservation. Everyone else thought it was the usual eruption. We wanted to protect our homes from the looting. Then the top of Vesuvius exploded."

Luna looks at the darkening sky. Ash and stone rain down and they stand in a cloud of dust. She closes her eyes and holds her breath, wishing she had an umbrella.

What a silly thing to wish for.

When she can't hold her breath any longer, Luna gasps, sucking in air. It's clean, even sweet. She opens her eyes.

A lady pours water across the street, a gecko caught up in its wave. On the sidewalk behind her, two men talk, the older one lifting the skirt of his toga to pee into a bucket.

Gross.

The air is no longer so sweet and she holds her breath again. They walk on faster, the spell broken. Valerius now looks like Natas, and she's back to being Frankie. But they're still in Pompeii.

"Is any of this real?"

"All of it is, from a time in your mind."

Frankie gives him a *stop-feeding-me-a-line* look. "You know what I mean. *Real* real."

"Well, of course not." He grimaces. "You know that, so why ask?"

"What is this, then?"

"Metaphors of our past existence; manifestations of our expectations; tools to make sense of what cannot otherwise be comprehended."

"Thanks for clearing that up."

"Sarcastic in every life."

"That's what people keep telling me."

Sarcasm: the essence of my soul. Frankie's okay with that.

"Can we visit other lives?"

"You are the one controlling your experience."

"I'm really not."

"Yet, you are."

Ahead, on top of a high pedestal, stands the bronze statue of Augustus riding his horse, his hand held out in salute. As a little girl, she'd stare up at the emperor's perfectly smooth face, at each defined ringlet of hair, and wonder, *Is this what he really looks like?*

Natas nods toward a narrow cobblestone street past the monument. "Home is that way. We should visit."

She follows him and—

Her foot!

Pulling it up, she draws a shard of broken pottery out from her heel. Blood follows, dripping onto the ash. Ash everywhere now, like a snowfall.

The pain is definitely real.

Why am I here? This isn't what I came to do.

"I need to get to Wilma," Frankie says. "Before she forgets. Before she dies."

Natas holds up a hand. "Don't worry, time does not exist here."

"That's so not true," Frankie says. "Why are you lying?"

Natas sighs. "We shall get to them soon."

They walk on in silence until they reach the veil—the actual veil Valerius taught behind. Anyone could come and hear him speak, but only after three years of being a Listener were you allowed to go to the other side and see his face. It was a serious power move.

Pushing the curtain aside, Natas walks down a set of stairs on the other side. Frankie follows him.

"Is this something we do every life?" Frankie asks, her voice and footsteps echoing. "We enter the Oblivion, and you guide me through it."

"No, Frances," Natas says. "This is something we have never done before."

62

Dörröppningar

How *does* time work in here? It feels like at least a day since she was down under the ruins, trying to separate. But if that were the case, wouldn't she need to sleep? *Can* you sleep in the Oblivion? What would you dream of here? The real world? Classes and friends and lunch?

The here Natas has led her to, however, seems all too real, even if there is no *here* here. No sea or shore, no city or forest, just a driving storm of flitting, writhing, terrified shadows, passing by one another—passing through one another—each trapped in their own miserable isolation, unaware that they're not alone. Frankie feels trapped inside a plastic bottle with every spirit she ever captured, and more. Many, many more.

"This no longer feels like a metaphor of whatever."

"It is not," Natas says. "This is the waiting room of souls."

"I don't want to stay here."

"No one does."

She remembers finding this place as a little girl and crying about it to Mama, who thought Luna was just having a nightmare. She also remembers coming here to rescue the Watson sisters, when they could no longer remember who they were.

They should seriously be thanking me.

Wanting to get away, Frankie walks faster, following Natas forward. She misses where they were before; she misses being Luna. She wants that salty sea breeze, wants her city back. And Marcellus. Poor, sweet, handsome Marcellus. *He loved me.* Luna believed he did anyway. How long did it take him to forget her, once he came inside the Oblivion? How many lives has he lived since then? The same sixty-six? Who is he now? A different handsome boy? Maybe she'd recognize his slightly pigeon-toed way of walking, the way he pouted his lips when he was thinking. But what if he's an ugly old man? Or a pine tree?

"Do people get reincarnated as trees?"

"No," Natas says.

Thank god. That would be seriously boring.

They arrive at the shore again. But how? They never turned around. All that walking, just to be back where they started.

It's like the time Frankie was in second grade and Mom dragged her and her brother around Ikea for hours, up and down escalators, through endless showrooms, and right when they finally got to checkout Lucie realized he forgot his stupid action figure in the bedding section—the *first* room—and he hysterically cried while Mom tried to trace the route back on the map and Frankie stamped her feet, refusing to walk all the way to the entrance. Then, a lady dressed in Ikea blue and gold appeared like a genie out of a bottle. "Don't worry, there's a secret door," she said. "A door that leads from the end to the beginning." She held it open, and it led right to the beds.

"Why don't you put this door on the map?" Frankie asked as Lucie ran to grab his action figure.

"Because they want you to see everything in the store."

Ikea: just like Hell.

Frankie looks out over the sea. She can't see that far, but she knows Wilma and Cadmus are on the opposite shore. All she has to do is walk across the water. That's all she ever had to do.

"Why did you take me in a circle?"

"Because you must not cross over," Natas says. "This is the point of no return. They are already lost."

"That's not true, either. I know it's not."

How she knows any of this, she can only take on faith.

"If you go, you risk forgetting. It has already started happening. You keep slipping away."

This is true.

"But I thought I was immune."

Natas shakes his head no. "The gift is not that you don't forget inside the Oblivion, it is that your memories return in your next life. If you stay in here too long, you will not remember to leave, and your life as Frankie will be lost. Your body will die, and you shall have to start all over again."

"I'm willing to take that chance."

"But **I** am not."

"Why?" Frankie says.

"I cannot bear to have you die right when you have come back, and to wait another fifteen years for you to awaken again. Besides," he says, raising an eyebrow and smiling, "I rather like this version of you." Natas holds out a hand for her to take. "Let us go back."

Moving her windswept hair away from her face, Frankie looks out over the sea.

"I can't give up on them just to save myself."

"Cadmus is going to die no matter what you do."

"And Wilma?"

"It is her choice."

"You don't care what happens to her?"

"Not particularly," Natas says. "And neither should you. She will be reborn as someone else."

"Someone *else*. Not the person I know."

Frankie starts walking on top of the water, splashing with each step.

"I have to stop you," Natas calls after her.

"I don't need your boosts to do this. Not at the lake, and definitely not in here."

But that's not what he means.

63
Metamorphoses

Frankie turns to look for Natas, but where did he go? She doesn't see the snake slithering across the surface of the water until it strikes, biting her on the ankle.

"Very poetic," Frankie says, wincing. "But I'm not Eurydice."

She grabs the serpent and flings it away. Midair, Natas changes into an eagle, climbs the air, banks, and swoops, poised to attack. Before he does, Frankie transforms herself into a hawk.

I guess I do control my lives in the Oblivion.

Attacking, Frankie rips a clump of feathers out of the eagle with her beak, and some flesh along with them.

It feels good.

Caw!

Against the backdrop of a threatening red sky, the two birds circle one another warily, each looking for an opening. Frustrated, Natas dives into the water. Frankie drops down, cruising just above the surface, searching for her prey. From the murky depths below, a shadow begins to emerge, getting larger. *Way* larger. Frankie flaps to gain altitude as a giant orca lunges out of the water, but she can't get high enough fast enough. The killer whale snatches the hawk in his jaws, dragging her down. Underwater, she shrinks herself into a needlefish to escape, and then expands into a dolphin.

Frankie loved her life as a dolphin. How fast she could swim. She puts more and more distance between herself and the pursuing orca. The joy of pushing through the water is even more exhilarating than flying through the air. So exhilarating that she loses track of where she is, and too late realizes she's swept up in a wave, crashing onto a rocky shore. She made it to the other side, only to thrash around helplessly as the water recedes. Before Frankie can regain her wits enough to change form, the orca beaches himself and sinks his jaws into her.

Pain: again, definitely real inside the Oblivion.

On the shore, she's human again, bleeding from her side. But where is her *actual* body?

The map in her brain—she can still sense inside the walls. Frankie locates herself down in the basement of the ruins at the very moment a spirit escapes through her eyes. The feeling is seriously unpleasant.

Frankie could return to her body right now, and have all this be over with.

That's what he wants me to do. Him, Natas, now a tiger prowling around her, huffing, nudging her. But Frankie can see his body, too, seated cross-legged, eyes rolled back, in his apartment.

My apartment.

"You're going to need to find another place to live."

"What are you doing?" Natas says.

He's no longer a tiger, but the shade of himself—and her father Valerius, and the Founder Ramakrishna, and that Victorian guy in the photo. Every other spirit shows only the faces of their most recent life—Natas has the faces of *hundreds* of lives.

"I'm sending you back home," she says. "I know you're concerned about me not remembering enough, so you'll be happy to know that I just recalled something very important." Dramatic pause. "I was always better at this than you."

"Remember not to—"

He never finishes the sentence. At least, not so Frankie hears.

Dr. Natas is locked back inside his body like a spirit in a bottle with the cap screwed on tight. He can't follow her anymore, and he certainly can't stop her.

There's one problem. The shore she crashed into isn't the other side after all. She crossed the sea just to come back to where she started. *Again.*

Except, now she isn't on the beach at all; she's not even outside. Instead, she's looking up at shelves of plates and silverware, a little girl surrounded by men and women arguing over napkin patterns and the agonized crying of babies desperate to leave.

"Is there just one magic door?" Frankie asks.

"Oh no," the nice lady in blue and gold says. "There are magic doors *all over* Ikea."

The door. They make it look like it's part of the wall. They don't want you to see it.

One thing Natas didn't lie about: This is the point of no return.

Eight-year-old Frankie walks through the door.

And comes out the other side as Mother.

64

Rescue

At last, she made it to the opposite shore. Off in the distance, down the beach, Cadmus and Wilma make sandcastles. He notices Frankie first.

"Mother!" he calls from afar. "Oh, Mother, I knew you'd come."

Dusting sand off his knees, Cadmus steps toward her. Not like when he needs a walker; like when he's up in the trees.

He throws his arms around her. "Welcome, welcome!"

"Welcome...," Frankie asks, "to where?"

"The Oblivion!" he says in an *of-course!* tone of voice. "Finally, I was able to make it this far. Isn't it beautiful?"

"What are **you** doing here?" Wilma shouts. Storming toward Frankie, Wilma knocks a sandcastle over. "Get away! Leave us alone!"

"It's okay, Wilma," Cadmus says. "Mother can't take us out. Not like she did with the sisters. We're too far in."

Is that true? Frankie searches for their bodies inside the walls, but where are they? She can't access the map inside her mind. This is the point of no return.

"Look at the water, Mother," Cadmus says, pointing. "It's Lethe. Whatever you do, don't drink from it, or you'll start to forget."

"I don't think that's how it works."

He looks at her, uncomprehending.

"Why did you come inside?" Frankie says to Cadmus. "You promised me you wouldn't."

"I made him come," Wilma says, getting between them.

"I'm sorry for disobeying you, Mother," Cadmus says, now an ashamed little boy, looking the same as when she would read to him.

"I'm not Mother," she says. "I'm Frankie."

"Frankie," he says. "Is that one of your other lives?"

He stares up at her with innocent sky-blue eyes and long blond eyelashes. Frankie can't bear it; why can't he go back to being an old man?

"Cadmus, we have to go," she says.

"Go where?"

"Back to the Institute."

"Oh no," he says. "No, we can't."

"Listen to me," Frankie says. "If we don't go, you'll die. Wilma will die. Your memories—they're getting erased."

Little boy Cadmus shakes his head violently no, closing his mouth hard like he'll burst into tears if he doesn't get what he wants.

"Stop doing this to him!" Wilma says, pulling Cadmus away from Frankie. "Don't you see you're making him cry?"

Frankie tries again to find the map inside her head—to force him back—but it's just not there.

"Wilma, forget being mad at me for one second," Frankie says. "If we don't leave now, we'll never be able to. And it won't stay pretty and peaceful like this. We'll forget everything we've ever known about ourselves, and we'll be like those spirits in the waiting room."

"What are you talking about?" Wilma says. "What waiting room?"

Frankie opens her mouth to explain, but she can't remember the question Wilma just asked. Desperate, she turns back to Cadmus.

"You got what you came for!" Frankie says. "Or you didn't—I don't know. Either way, staying longer won't help. We have to *go!*"

Cadmus suddenly returns to his old man self, barely able to stand, shaking. "What is it I came for again?"

"The gift, Grandpa!" Wilma says. "Don't you remember?"

Cadmus stares at her blankly, his eyes colorless, his skin translucent.

A look of horror comes over Wilma's face.

"We're going to die in here, Frankie," Wilma says, panicked. "We're all going to die!"

"Calm down," Frankie says. "We both have to calm down. It has to be like we're back in our room."

"Back in our room . . . ," Wilma repeats, nodding.

"Let's sit down here, on the sand," Frankie says, holding up a hand to pull Wilma down to face her. "Close your eyes, and remember when you taught me to levitate."

Wilma nods her head, her bangs falling across her pressed-shut eyelids. She pulls her feet into her knees, and Frankie does the same.

Just like they did all spring semester, the two of them rise; what Frankie realizes now that she didn't understand then is that they lift each other.

In her mind, Frankie feels Wilma's presence. Not here in the Oblivion, but inside the walls, down under the ruins of the Boathouse. She can sense their bodies again.

"What are you doing?" Cadmus says, his voice shaky.

"Leaving."

As Frankie says the word, they're gone.

65

Saturday

Where am I? Opening her eyes, all she sees is blackness. Frankie tries to remember what was happening outside of the Oblivion, and realizes today must be Saturday. The day they go home—right! She can't wait. Flemington has never sounded so good.

But Mom and Lucie! They must be looking for her—it must be time to leave. Except, what time *is* it? It's too dark down here to tell.

"Wilma, where are you?" she calls out. "Cadmus? Are you guys here?"

Did they already levitate through the fallen doorway? Frankie looks up, but there's no opening above her.

Her eyes adjust to the darkness enough to be able to make out shapes. Everything seems orderly. *That's not right.* There are no toppled tanks or chunks of rubble, and the staircase is upright again. The basement is back to how it was before the fire.

Climbing the stairs, she grips on to the handrail. At the top, she pushes the door open and lays eyes on what she hasn't seen in thirty years.

The Boathouse.

She wanders the big airy room, taking it in. The rowing shells they had from the sanatorium days are long gone but the old canoe, the one with the hole in it, still hangs on the wall. *We always said we would fix it*, she thinks as she runs her hand over the waxy wood hull. The big double doors that give out onto the dock are open and she has to squint, the sunlight glinting off the lake is so bright.

She smiles.

Did she travel through time? Can you go into the Oblivion and come out in a different year?

She doesn't want to leave the Boathouse, worried this somehow isn't real, that the building will vanish. *It's so lovely to be here.*

Outside, on the dock, her friends are having a picnic. Oh, right! Because today is Saturday. How wonderful to be a Saturday!

On a blanket, Penny feeds grapes to Lonnie. Laughing, she gets up and runs away, Lonnie throwing a grape after her. Penny is so young. She looks just like she did in that movie, the one about the swamp creature. And Lonnie! His ponytail is far more flattering at this age. The suspenders—well, they've always looked atrocious.

Penny stops to wave at a passing boat on the lake. Shielding her eyes, Diana waves back while Fred rows. Right, Fred! How could she *not* remember Fred? He was such a decent young man. The others, they could be so self-involved, but not Fred.

Daring to lean her head out of the Boathouse doorway, she sees Cadmus. He's lean and muscly, swinging Wilma in circles with long outstretched arms. She can't be more than three. He lets go and she giggles, stumbling around, dizzy. His dancing blue eyes follow her as she runs off to play with other children. Then, Cadmus turns.

"You were right that we should leave, Mother," he says.

"How is Wilma here?" she says. "She hasn't been born yet."

"Oh, that's not Wilma," he says, looking over to the girl, playing. "That's Sohui, her mother."

Right, of course.

"Wilma does look just like her."

Cadmus's demeanor changes, his forehead buckling in concern. "Have you checked on the Founder yet?" he asks.

"No, I haven't."

Scolding herself, Mother walks back into the Boathouse and up the stairs. Paintings brighten the wood-paneled hallway of the second floor, watercolors of the lake that friends painted decades ago. *So many talented friends.* The door to the front bedroom is ajar; she pushes it farther in.

"Is that you, Mother?" the Founder says, his breathing shallow and labored.

"Go back to sleep."

"I am so cold..."

"You left the window open, silly man."

Draping a blanket over him, she notices his bones poking through his bedclothes, his rib cage expanding and collapsing with each breath. How could the Founder get to this point? Ramakrishna was so strong when he came to get her that rain-soaked morning in Shanghai. *Of course, we always get to this point.*

Shutting the window, Mother throws open the curtains, letting the light in. Dust dances in the sunbeam. Outside, Penny and Diana jump into the water to join Fred. Lonnie retreats to the middle of the dock, trying not to get wet, but Penny climbs out and grabs his arm. He shakes his head *no no no*, pulling his arm back, but can't resist her. Sohui, now in Cadmus's arms, points down at them, splashing and laughing.

When were they happy like this? When were they *young* like this? It wasn't when the Founder was sick. Why is it later here inside the Boathouse?

Mother can't stay in this room that reeks of death. She despises the end of life, the helplessness of it, the long, grieving goodbyes. She wants to be diving off the dock, eating grilled corn, finishing that jigsaw puzzle they were working on—the one of the Great Wall.

I love it here, Mother thinks, walking down the hallway. *I'm so happy to be home.*

"Frankie?" a voice travels up the stairwell.

She freezes on the top step.

"Frankie, is that you?"

Who is *Frankie*?

Descending slowly to the bottom of the stairs, she finds Estelle and Mitzi.

The Watson sisters.

66

Hopeless

Is it time for their lesson already? These young ladies, they're so talented. They won't be scholars, lord knows, but the way they channel, they might turn out to be even more powerful than Cadmus.

But what they will do. What they will ruin! She *shouldn't* teach them.

"Frankie, we have to go," Estelle says.

"I know you want to go inside the Oblivion, but you mustn't," Mother says to them. "All this will be destroyed if you do. *He* will die." Mother points up to the Founder's bedroom. "Promise me you won't."

"Frankie, that already happened," Mitzi says.

"Why do you keep calling me by that name?"

"We're here to take you out of the Oblivion, dear," Estelle says.

"Me?"

"Frankie—you're stuck inside," Mitzi says.

"No, I dragged *you* out, like I just dragged out Cadmus. To the good times, so we can all be happy."

"These *were* good times," Estelle says.

"Shut up, sister," Mitzi says. "You're not helping."

"This is good for the both of you, as well," Mother says. "You have a second chance. You don't have to make the same mistake."

"We can talk about this later," Estelle says, talking to her slowly, like she's some kind of idiot. "But we have to go. And you must *want* to go."

"We're not strong enough to force you out of the Oblivion," Mitzi says.

"Stop saying that!" Mother says. "You two can't enter the Oblivion. I trapped you in your bodies, in the gym. You'll die if you leave. I'm sorry I had to but I couldn't trust you—it was for your own good. We're in the past, so you don't know what happened yet."

"She's gone," Mitzi whispers to her sister. *"There's no hope."*

"Natas already tried to bring you back, but you sent *him* back, and trapped him there," Estelle says loudly, as if Mother were hard of hearing as well as stupid. "That's why he freed us."

"Which he was supposed to have done *months* ago," Mitzi says. "We had a deal!"

"Sister, please!" Estelle says. "Can't you see we're about to lose this girl?"

"What do we even care?" Mitzi throws up her hands. "We're free."

"But look at her," Estelle says. "She's a pathetic shell of a human being! The poor child can't even remember she's Frankie. She's about to die."

The bickering—she can't forget their bickering. When they taught her. When she found the crystals. *When they made me clean the drains in the boy's shower.*

Frankie rubs her face, squeezing her eyes shut tight. *Yes, yes, I remember.* Sending Natas back, traveling with Cadmus and Wilma to the basement. Except they never made it there.

"The seduction of the Oblivion isn't immortality, but nostalgia," Mother told Cadmus when she made him swear never to go in. *"It's getting lost in your memories before they are wiped away forever."*

When Frankie opens her eyes, she's back on the shore.

The sisters are gone.

"Frankie! Frankie!" Wilma comes running to her. "Where have you *been*?" she says. "Grandpa is sick—he's not talking! He's in the water!"

Frankie follows Wilma to where the waves pound the beach, and there's Cadmus, lying in the foaming sea. Wilma takes hold of one of his arms.

"Grab the other one! We have to pull him out!"

Wilma's trying to drag him but he won't budge. The surf seethes around his body.

"Wilma, we *all* have to go," Frankie says.

Inside of her mind, the map is back; she can feel her body. For real, this time.

The sea is gone. Instead of water, shadows seethe around them; they're just three random spirits among the desperate millions. *The waiting room of souls.* Shadows pierce through Frankie. She feels herself slipping away again. Fear of annihilation surges within her, crushing every thought.

Omnia mutantur nihil interit

Calming herself enough, Frankie grabs hold of Wilma and sends her spiraling out of the Oblivion; her body hungrily sucks her soul back in. Next, she grabs Cadmus, but when she tries to return him to his body, his spirit won't fit. Frankie needs to take him back a different way—through *her* body. She left the door open, after all.

Seizing Cadmus, she lets the magnetic attraction between soul and body take over. The two shadows travel across the breach in an instant.

Frankie opens her eyes. She's in the basement.

But am I really?

Uncrossing her legs to stand up, Frankie staggers and falls. Both her legs are asleep, and the cramp of hunger in the pit of her stomach makes her double over. *Definitely out of the Oblivion this time.* Getting back up, Frankie finds she's not alone.

Sun streams through the fallen doorway in a column, bathing Wilma in light. She's kneeling over her grandfather, his body awkwardly splayed on the ground, limp. Looming above them, a stark black form resists the sunbeam: the shadow of Cadmus.

"Frankie! Frankie!" Wilma turns to her, wailing. "Put him back in!"

She tries, but his body might as well be stone. There's no place inside of it for a spirit to go.

Cadmus is dead.

Wilma weeps, hugging her grandfather's body.

It's okay, Wilma, the Cadmus shadow says. *I'm still here.*

"Did it work?" Wilma looks up at the spirit. "Will you come back?"

Maybe I will. He turns to Frankie. *I still remember who I am.*

"Frankie—did it work?" Wilma asks, rubbing tears away.

Frankie nods. "It worked. He'll remember."

The shade turns to Frankie, all of his faces visible simultaneously—young, old, and in between.

Make sure that my body is cremated, the spirit says, looking down to his corpse. *I don't want to come back to a skull.*

"You have to go," Frankie says. Then to Wilma. "He has to go so he can come back."

Standing, Wilma looks into the eyes of her grandfather's spirit. Her own are red with tears.

There will be no goodbye, Wilma.

If she expected something dramatic—the spirit of Cadmus rising through the fallen doorway to the sky or his shadow gently fading into the warm light of the Oblivion—it doesn't happen. He's just gone.

Frankie holds Wilma, crying harder.

"Are you sure he'll come back?"

"Sure I'm sure," Frankie says.

Of course, the truth is that Frankie has no idea.

67

Ravenous

"You need to slow down. You're going to make yourself ill if you continue eating like that," Mr. Silvenus says.

"So I was inside for *three* days?" Frankie asks again.

Dr. Natas nods.

"I can't believe you freed the sisters to get me out," Frankie says to Dr. Natas. "You really do care about me, Rudy."

Dr. Natas ignores the Rudy comment.

"It was *my* idea to free the Watson sisters. This one was just moping," Mr. Silvenus says, gesturing toward Dr. Natas. "At one point, I thought he wanted to let you die."

Frankie swallows her food so she can speak. "So, Lucie didn't wait around to see what happened to me? And not my mom either?"

Typical.

"It is not as if they knew where you were," Dr. Natas says.

"What'd you tell them?"

"That you ran away again," Mr. Silvenus says.

"And they believed it?" Frankie says.

The two men look at each other, then at her. *Be serious.*

"Yeah, I guess that tracks." Frankie finishes the last of the veggie burger in a single bite. "You have any more of these?"

"You already ate the whole box."

"There were only two."

Mr. Silvenus sighs, getting up. "Let me make you some toast."

"So . . . it's just the three of us? And Wilma?" Frankie says, looking to the guest room where Wilma is sleeping. She practically collapsed when they got here.

"Yes," Dr. Natas says.

"How about the sisters?"

"Gone."

"Already?"

"After thirty-five years in that gym, I believe they would dispute the term *already*," Mr. Silvenus calls from the kitchen. "And it isn't like *he* wanted them to stay."

"I gave them a vehicle."

"The Jaguar?" Frankie says.

"Hardly," Dr. Natas says. "I let them take the van."

"They should be back in Canada by now," Mr. Silvenus says. "They left last night."

"It was *yesterday* that I saw them inside?" Frankie says. "Time works that differently?"

Dr. Natas nods.

"So," Frankie says as the toaster pops, "what do we do now?"

68

One Month Later

"**You sure have** been doing a lot of traveling this summer, sis," Lucie says. "Times Square, LA, Hell, Arizona. How does Sedona compare to the multiverse?"

"I keep telling you, the Oblivion is nothing like some stupid super-hero movie."

They're seeing each other for the first time since two weeks ago, when Frankie left Flemington to fly to Arizona for Cadmus's memorial. They've never been apart this long before.

"Where should I put this?" Lucie says, holding the handle of his rolling suitcase.

"You're taking that one," Frankie says, pointing to Dr. Natas's old bedroom.

"So, he's really gone?"

Frankie nods.

"He's probably in Tokyo with Ek by now," she says.

"And he's no longer, like, going to run the school?"

"He's still the head of the school," Frankie says. "Technically."

"But *you* are going to run it," Lucie says in his *let-me-see-if-I've-got-this-right* voice. "I know you remember sixty-five past lives, but in this one, you're still fourteen. You being the principal—it's beyond weird."

"What do you want me to do, Lucie? Go back to school?" Frankie says. "Mother came up with half of the curriculum. I know the answers."

Except in calculus. She wonders if there was ever a life she was good in math.

"Don't be such an idiot, bro!" some kid shouts on the stairwell.

"Shut up!" a different kid says.

The students have been coming back all day. She saw Mistral this morning, and told him about her becoming the new "student principal" of the school. Even with the euphemistic title, he didn't like it any more than Lucie.

"So what am I supposed to call you? *Miss Caridi?* And why are *you* moving into the principal's office? Because you're a witch?"

The two of them are right, obviously—it *is* super weird to have a kid who's supposed to be a freshman suddenly run the school.

Which is exactly what Frankie said to Dr. Natas.

"When I was fifteen, I was at Harvard doing groundbreaking research on the human genome," he said. "I'm quite confident *you* can run this remote little outpost of classical education. Besides, the school was your dream. I have merely been minding it until your return."

Frankie came to his office expecting him and Mr. Silvenus to explain how the place operated—and where to find two new gym teachers—but instead Dr. Natas brought a stack of passports out of a wall safe. A British one for a person named "Doris Feldman" has her photo in it.

"Why'dja name me Doris, didja? I don't look like a *Doris*," Frankie said in her best Eliza Doolittle accent. "And 'owdja get this picture a me?"

"From your school ID," Mr. Silvenus said. "And please never do that voice again."

There's also an Australian passport for her, and an Irish one, plus more for Dr. Natas and Mr. Silvenus.

"Why do we need fake passports?" Frankie asked.

"To flee," Dr. Natas said. "When the townspeople storm the gates."

"I don't think Dink and Mr. Zorn are going to come after us with torches and pitchforks."

"Do not be so sure," Dr. Natas said. "Our backup plans prove to be lifesaving all too often."

What most surprised Frankie was the money.

"What money?" she said.

"You remember how to hunt mice from the skies and the names of every fishmonger in 79 AD, but you never remember the money," Dr. Natas said, shaking his head.

"We possess one of the largest fortunes on Earth," Mr. Silvenus said eagerly.

She doesn't know about in her past lives, but Frankie is definitely interested in the money in this one.

"So," Frankie said, now herself with the *let-me-see-if-I've-got-this-right* voice. "Are you guys saying we're rich?"

"Fantastically," Mr. Silvenus said.

"The only power I have ever discovered to be greater than that of channeling," Dr. Natas said, "is money."

"Hey, I need money," Frankie said. "Can I have money?"

"You're not old enough."

"What happened to running the genome project at Harvard at my age? Didn't Mother give you an allowance or something?" she said. "Didn't *I* give you an allowance?"

The money, it turns out, isn't just money. There are silver and gold bars stashed in safety-deposit boxes from Switzerland to New Zealand, jewelry and gems buried in Iranian caves and bricked up inside of adobe walls in Mexico.

"Plus the real estate!" Mr. Silvenus said. "The 1800s were the right time to buy property in London. Not to mention New York."

As for how they manage it all, that's where the Mysterions come in. The investment company they work for, Sibylla, has a single client.

"Us."

Sibylla is based in Tokyo, which is the real reason Dr. Natas moved there.

When he was packing to go, Frankie was surprised that she really didn't want him to. Especially considering what he had done to Cadmus.

"What you *think* I did to him," Dr. Natas said.

It took Frankie a couple of days. Only when she walked past the grave of the sheep did she realize.

"I know you did it."

"Three days without food and water," Dr. Natas said. "How could the old man have possibly survived?"

"Do you deny killing Fred?" Frankie said.

"Must we start *that* again?" he said. "I told Mother a thousand times that I did not murder Fred."

"So you're telling me you've never killed anyone?"

"Of course I have," Dr. Natas said, putting shirts in his suitcase. "This very life, I killed my so-called father. He should never have beat my mother, and certainly not me."

This was alarming.

"You did that thing you did to the sheep," Frankie said, "to your *father*?"

"What I did to the sheep was nothing more than a blood clot in the brain, quite easy when you know both telekinesis and mammalian anatomy. But no," Dr. Natas said. "We lived far from any breach, so I had to do it the old-fashioned way."

"How?" Frankie asked. "You were only eight."

"Use your imagination. I will simply tell you that the man deserved a more painful death than the one he received." Dr. Natas snapped his suitcase shut and pulled it off the bed. "Out of necessity, you have done the same thing. You get born a woman—well, mostly you do—so you have had it far worse than I."

Now it's Lucie with a suitcase on the same bed, unpacking. Except he hasn't started yet.

"Are you sure you want me to be your roommate?" he says.

"I don't want to live alone in this big apartment." It isn't that big, but still.

"What if Wilma decides to come back?" Lucie says.

"Wilma's not family."

Frankie smiles, and Lucie smiles back. He unzips his suitcase.

"How's she doing?" Lucie asks, opening up the top drawer of the dresser.

"Pretty good, actually."

Frankie stayed with Wilma the week of the memorial service, which took place in the high Arizona desert of Sedona.

The event wasn't put together by Wilma's grandmother, but Cadmus's more recent ex-wife. Hundreds of people attended the ceremony, most of them his former students. Lonnie and Diana came with Penny, as did one other person Frankie knew. With her gray hair dyed red and the new clothes, however, she was unrecognizable. Until she spoke.

"Hello, Frankie," the woman said.

Frankie felt her jaw drop. *"Not-Estelle?"*

"Call me Mitzi." She smiled. "All my friends do."

When Frankie asked where Estelle was, Mitzi said that her sister met a guy before they even made it across the border. "They're on a road trip in his camper," she said. "We needed a break from each other, anyway."

When the service was done, mourners lined up to take ashes

to spread in the desert. It was nice that Cadmus got his wish to be cremated. (He'd get his other wish, too. As for how Frankie managed to put the spirits back inside the Oblivion, that's a whole other story.)

Taking a handful, Frankie was surprised by how dense it was—more like the ash from Pompeii than a campfire. She was glad to do this; it might not have been digging a grave, but releasing Cadmus's ashes to the breeze was cathartic all the same.

Watching the tiny particles float away, Frankie couldn't imagine a better final resting place. Cathedral Rock looked as fantastical as anything inside the Oblivion. Frankie could detect a faint breach here, too; Ruby White Wolf was right about this being a place with more power than New Jersey. Not like inside the walls—she had one bar of signal, max—but enough to push a pea across a plate.

It was when they got back to her house that Wilma told Frankie she was going to stay in Arizona.

"For a little while."

"You're not coming back to school?"

Her grandmother needed help, Wilma said. "Grandpa didn't leave her anything." She shrugged. "It turns out he *was* pretty selfish."

Lucie smiles, hearing Frankie tell the story.

"Do you think Cadmus will be able to come back? I mean, to remember," he says, putting socks in a drawer.

"I don't know, but I guess we'll find out," Frankie says. "In 2040 something."

For Frankie, the question isn't if Cadmus will remember his past life, but whether Wilma will. Because maybe it's not how far inside the Oblivion you make it or how long you stay, but how young you are when you go. The idea makes Frankie happy, that she and Wilma could keep finding each other, life after life.

With Dr. Natas, it's more complicated.

"We have to talk about you being my father," Frankie said.

"First, I am *not* your father. Valerius was Luna's father, and that is a very different thing," Dr. Natas said, putting his luggage in the trunk of the convertible. "Second, I refuse to engage on this subject in yet another life."

Frankie gritted her teeth at being dismissed, accepting it only because she had a more important question to ask.

"Are you Pythagoras?"

Dr. Natas brushed by her, opening the driver's-side door.

"I will never tell you. Not in this life"—door slam—"nor any other."

"That means you definitely aren't," Frankie said. "Because if you were? Boom, mic drop."

Dr. Natas smiled. A real smile, for once. "It hardly means that at all," he said, starting the car. "Whatever what you just said means."

Now, Lucie slides his empty suitcase under the bed.

"Well, that's it. I'm officially roommates with my sister," he says. "And Mother. And like twenty other people."

"Shut up," Frankie says.

Because she really is just Frankie. She might share memories with Luna and Mother, but their narratives are all different. What they believe in, too. Like how Mother told Cadmus that eternal memory isn't a gift. Sure, it's sad to remember Marcellus from back in Pompeii, and to think of how her mother and sisters died. But she's lucky to have known them, and to be able to keep them alive in her memories.

Remembering your past lives isn't a curse.

It's freaking amazing.

EPILOGUE

"Hey, Mr. S.!"

"Why, greetings to you as well, Mr. Riojas," Silvenus says, pausing in the halls to shake the young man's hand. "I do hope you have come back from your summer holiday energized and ready to learn!"

"You know it."

Silvenus does love the return of students for fall semester, when the halls of school once again resound with the vibrant hum of youthful chatter. It puts the Latin teacher in a splendid mood as he unlocks the room that remains his favorite on campus.

Ah, the smell of old books! How he does adore a library. With Ms. Castillo not due in for another hour, Silvenus has the place to himself. All the same, he turns the lock on the door behind him, to be sure.

The old satyr passes through the stacks, pleased with how everything has turned out. To have Frankie well on the road to recovering her memories *and* Natas on another continent? Endings scarcely turn out better than this.

Of course, Natas was duplicitous to the last. He told Frankie he was "minding" the school; mining it is more the truth. Students such as Ekwueme are his true prized jewels; the young man believes that by following his mentor he is entering a life of service, but his life will be *in* service, to Natas himself.

And Oxnard. Natas played that one perfectly. The man's eternal genius lies in knowing how to feed the egoistic needs of others. Oxnard yearns to be an insider, so Natas pretends to take him under his wing—to tell him "secrets"—and now the boy will do anything for him.

Moira, Efrat, and even Lucius will all come to serve him in one way or the other, as every one of the Listeners have. Except Cadmus. Cadmus always stood apart. A shame he died.

Oh, well.

At the back of the library, Silvenus takes a different key from the ring and reaches his hand behind the bookcase marked *Ancient Architecture*. He fumbles to fit the key into the lock, twists it, and moves the bookcase ever so slightly. The old satyr glances back to make absolutely sure he is alone, then slips into the room.

The *gabinetto segreto*, Mother called it. A secret chamber to house her masterpiece. Now, where is the light switch? Here.

Before he left, Natas took the time to criticize Silvenus for telling Frances too much about her past lives. He's not wrong. Silvenus has always been an "oversharer," as his students say. And Mother herself told Silvenus to take it slowly with her next incarnation.

"So much of the past is too disturbing for a young woman to hear, especially those of today," she said. "It's too disturbing even for me, at my age."

Mother told this to Silvenus when they were feeding the sheep together. It must have been thirty years ago. The sheep were her idea; she always loved animals. There was an Argus then, too.

Which life was it that she first had a dog named Argus?

Silvenus runs his fingers over the spines of the clothbound volumes of the *gabinetto segreto*. The 55th, the 56th, the 57th, the 57th, still the 57th—so many volumes of that one—Yes! Here it is.

The 58th Rebirth of Helene Margot.

Silvenus draws the book from the shelf and begins to leaf through its pages. He immediately gets lost in her words, forgetting why he picked out this life in the first place.

It *is* a good one. Shocking, really.

Mother was right, Silvenus thinks to himself. Frankie might have been ready to go inside the Oblivion, but she isn't ready to come in here.